The Whiskey Wagon

The old drunk felt that he was in paradise when the whiskey wagon turned up. Whereas the preacher was horrified – until he learned how valuable it was. Other people had different views. The marshal of Huyton township wanted to know who owned it, while local businessmen fought over the cargo.

Then things got worse. The old drunk went missing and the wagon disappeared, while the local gun store was raided. Bounty hunters came into town, and one of them was on the prod.

It all erupted with shoot-outs and a lynching, as all the respectable citizens fell under suspicion. When would the blood stop flowing?

The Whiskey Wagon

Tom Benson

A Black Horse Western

ROBERT HALE · LONDON

ISBN 0 7090 7604 5

Robert Hale Limited
Clerkenwell House
Clerkenwell Green
London EC1R 0HT

Typeset by
Derek Doyle & Associates, Liverpool.
Printed and bound in Great Britain by
Antony Rowe Limited, Wiltshire

ONE

The preacher made the journey every Sunday. After breathing hellfire and damnation to his own congregation in the little town of Huyton, he then took the ten-mile trip to the lumber camp up near Danver's Creek. It was not something that the loggers looked forward to, but their boss had been persuaded by his wife that it would be good for their souls to have regular visits from a reverend spreader of eternal happiness.

Obadiah Scrubbs was not everybody's idea of such a heavenly herald. He was tall, thin as a bean-pole, and wore a sour expression that terrified women who had milk in their kitchens. His white hair grew wild and straggly above the lined face, and his clothes were always a rusty black. He was seldom seen without a Bible ready for opening with an appropriate quotation.

He travelled in a small surrey, driven by old Fred who sat silently throughout the long journey. He contemplated the moment when he would be paid off and could retire to the saloon to spend the money on the better things of life.

Fred Brown was short and fat, his face reddish around the button nose, and his eyes dulled by the years and the consumption of cloudy beer and cheap whiskey. He did odd jobs around the town, lived in a little hut behind the schoolma'am's house, and was now enjoying the few years he had left. He never believed one word of the doom and gloom that Obadiah preached, but he also had a shrewd suspicion that neither did Obadiah.

It was a weary journey back from the logging camp. Night had fallen and the sky was overcast with rain threatening as the wind blew in fitful gusts. The horse moved slowly, picking its way over the uneven trail, and Fred was beginning to get a little nervous as flashes of lightning cut across the clouds to the south.

Obadiah had noticed it too and leaned over to his companion.

'Go through the canyon,' he said in his grating voice.

The driver nearly dropped the reins.

'It's too dangerous,' he protested nervously. 'Bad enough in broad daylight, preacher, but with all them ghosts about . . . !'

'Rubbish, man. There ain't no such thing as ghosts. They're the evil images created by feeble minds. It'll take half an hour or more off the journey.'

Fred swallowed noisily.

6

'All them Yankee soldiers was killed there durin' the war,' he protested. 'Folks in these parts don't go near the place.'

'Superstitious nonsense, man. Get on with it. I aim to be in my bed before midnight.'

Fred clamped his lips tightly shut and did as he was told. The mouth of the small canyon was reached about ten minutes later and he reluctantly headed the surrey between its confining walls.

Rain was beginning to fall now and thunder could be heard in the distance. The canyon lay between two low buttes that would otherwise have to be skirted. It was true that local people always preferred the longer way round despite the quick half-mile dash between the greyish walls of crumbling stone. It was not really because of the massacre twenty years earlier, but more due to the regular falls of rock that could be dangerous or might block the trail.

The sides of the canyon were lined with cacti and tall bushes that threw out windswept branches to brush against the sides of the surrey as it passed. Fred had to keep a tight rein on the horse in case some touching piece of foliage spooked it in the darkness.

A flash of lightning lit up the scene for a moment and the animal reared in fright. Old Fred cursed and the preacher called on divine intervention. Then the night darkened again and thunder came from the distant hills. Old Fred had stopped the surrey and sat as if glued to his seat.

'Get on with it, man!' Obadiah bawled at him. 'You have the Lord protectin' you.'

'I seen something, Preacher,' the old man muttered fearfully. 'In them bushes.'

He pointed over to the right where a screen of cholla was swaying slightly with a creaking that could be heard in the silence following the thunder. Obadiah peered into the gloom and opened his mouth to castigate the driver. Then he saw it too.

There was a wagon hidden among the foliage. He could just make out the hooped canvas cover and a pair of shafts that stretched out in front. Another flash of lightning lit up the scene and the harness could be discerned in a heap on the ground. It was quite a small wagon to be pulled by a single horse and appeared to be in pretty new condition.

'Well, it ain't your ghosts,' the preacher said with a certain cheerfulness. 'Let's go take a look.'

He got down from the surrey and was hastily joined by Fred, who did not fancy being left alone. They pushed their way through the tall growth and stood at the rear of the wagon. The canvas was drawn tight with leather straps that kept away both bad weather and prying eyes.

'Open it up,' the preacher ordered.

The old man hesitated for a moment, then reached for the leather straps and the large brass buckles. His shaking fingers took a while to undo the things, but when he drew back the canvas, no

8

demons or ghosts came out to carry him off to hell. He peered inside the wagon, resting his hands on the tailboard.

'Jumpin' Jehosaphat!' he exclaimed as a distant flash of lightning added a little light to the scene. 'It's whiskey!'

'Whiskey!' The preacher's use of the word was like a sentence of death. His bitter face contracted in hatred of the very commodity that lay before him.

Fred felt in his waistcoat pocket and took out a vesta-box. He struck a match and held it up to see what prize was unfolding before his suddenly happy eyes.

There were barrels, boxes, and jars of the stuff. Some bore famous names, and there were crates of brandy-bottles lying between two large glass containers which were enclosed in wire frames. Everything on the wagon appeared to be strong liquor.

'How in hell's name did it get here!' the old man asked in bewilderment.

The preacher ignored the language and took a deep breath. It was the way he usually started one of his hell-fire sermons. He placed both hands up to the lapels of his frock-coat.

'It is the work of the Almighty, Fred,' he intoned piously. 'You and me has the privilege of bein' his chosen ones. This consignment of Hell's brew has been delivered into the hands of the righteous for destruction.'

9

'Destruction!' The old man reeled back against the wagon. 'You aim to destroy all this, Preacher?'

'I aim to burn this load of corruption to save poor, benighted souls from their own evil ways. Smash some of those brandy-bottles and throw the liquid over the wagon. It will burn like an avenging fury and cleanse the canyon and the world of another evil.'

Fred stood for a moment with the burnt-out vesta in his fingers. He was doing some fast thinking and it was as well that Obadiah could not see the workings of his face in the darkness.

'Y'know, Preacher,' he said slowly, 'it could just be that some trader had an accident with his horse and has had to leave this stuff here until he can get another animal. If we destroy it, we sure as hell would be breakin' the law.'

'The work of the Almighty is above the law, Fred.'

'Judge Mason won't think that way, Preacher,' Fred assured him. 'And he ain't a friend of your'n nohow.'

It seemed to halt Obadiah in his stride, and that gave Fred time for a further sally.

'And another thing, Preacher,' he said quietly. 'There must be quite a loada money tied up in this. You'd have to pay for what you destroyed. The court would be right tough about that. Them fellas on juries tend to like their drink.'

Obadiah let his hands fall from the lapels and Fred knew that he was winning the argument.

'And then,' he added craftily, 'supposin' as how there ain't no claim for this wagon. It would be right foolish to waste all that liquor when it could be sold off to make money for your preachin' mission.'

There was a long silence, marred only by distant thunder and the movements of their horse in the background.

'You might have the right of it there, Fred,' the preacher conceded. 'Those who drink this vile stuff will only find another route to perdition. But if we used the money wisely, there are many souls to be saved in this sad world of ours. I think I have a solution.'

He tapped the side of the wagon with a bony finger.

'We will go back to town, get ourselves a draught-animal, and come back here to collect this wagon. We will put it in my barn where no wilful and weak creatures are likely to find it, and then we will wait, Fred. We will wait until it is claimed. If that does not happen, we can sell the contents and use the money for the saving of souls. That would be the way the Almighty would wish it.'

'Amen to that, Preacher,' Fred said thankfully. 'There is just one thing though. Suppose it ain't what it seems?'

Obadiah Scrubbs frowned at the little man.

'And what do you mean by that?' he asked sternly.

'Well, now, Preacher,' Fred explained with a

straight face, 'it could be that this load of stuff is part of some flim-flam. It could be coloured water, bein' taken somewheres to trick a parcel of rubes outa their money. We don't want to go haulin' coloured water back to town, do we?'

Obadiah nodded. 'You'd better check on it, Fred,' he said with judicial solemnity.

The old man lowered the tailboard and scrambled up on to the wagon with amazing alacrity. He chose a stone jar of the cheaper whiskey and soon had the top off with the aid of his knife. The preacher watched while he raised it to his nose, smelled the contents carefully, and then took a long swig. His face was bathed in a beatific smile as he smacked his lips and had another pull at the jug.

'It's the real thing, Preacher,' he said happily as he reached down to offer the jug to his companion. A bony arm waved away the jar with a contemptuous gesture.

'Well, that bein' settled,' Obadiah ordained, 'we will go to town and get ourselves a horse.'

'You'll need a pretty heavy animal,' old Fred said thoughtfully. 'Phil Breen's got some at his livery stable, but I reckon him as bein' just about the most talkative man in town. Besides, he'll be in bed by the time we get to Huyton.'

The preacher nodded his head slowly.

'We could borrow it,' he said. 'Phil need never know.'

'Is that honest, Preacher?'

Obadiah Scrubbs drew himself up majestically.

'It's for the work of the Lord, Fred,' he said proudly, 'and that justifies usin' methods that keep wrong-headed folk like Phil Breen in the dark about our doings. Now, let's get aboard the surrey and head for town. We've got to get this stuff stowed away before daybreak.'

They were on their way again a few minutes later. Fred had the jar tucked safely under the seat and he drove as fast as possible while the rain began to spatter in large drops that sparkled in the lightning flashes. It was the first rain of the year; maybe the only rain, and tomorrow would see the parched earth sprouting new growth.

Huyton was a small town with one main street, several side lanes, a few stores, and a saloon that thrived on the timber business that was fast ruining the lower slopes of the hills, and eroding the soil. The schoolhouse and the preacher's larger residence were at the bottom end of the main street. A small mission hall stood next to the burial ground on a flat area that bordered the creek.

Fred stopped the surrey behind the preacher's home, tethered the horse to the corral rail, and then followed his boss along another lane to the large corral behind the livery stable. There were a dozen horses there and several mules. They were all gathered together in the lea of a shed to shelter from the rain, and looked too miserable to take any notice of the two men who approached silently.

13

The rooms over the livery stable were in darkness, as were all the buildings around. Obadiah opened the gate and walked through the muddy corral to stand in front of the animals. He picked a sturdy horse and grabbed it firmly by the headband. It followed him with all the docility of a draught-animal as he headed back for the gate. Fred waited nervously, ready to close up the corral again.

The preacher and the horse passed through. Fred drew the large gate silently across, and was just about to fasten it, when a shotgun blasted the night air and the horse bolted.

TWO

They were all talking at once. Ma Breen banged the butt of her shotgun on the floor of the jail-house while her husband, sleepy and drunk, tried to take it off her. Old Fred and the preacher stood sheepishly in front of the marshal's desk as the lawman patiently waited for the fuss to die down. Mayor Kroner sat at the marshal's side, his heavy face set in a judicial scowl.

'I thought they was thieves,' the sturdy woman shouted. 'With all this thunder and lightning goin' on, I couldn't sleep. His snorin' didn't help none either. And then I hears this noise, looks outa the window, and here's these two fellas takin' old Bess outa the corral. So I blazed away.'

'You might have killed us,' the preacher protested angrily. 'I don't go around rustlin' horses, madam. We was borrowin' the animal.'

'If I'd wanted to kill you, Preacher,' the woman snorted, 'I'd not have missed. I fired into the air to scare the hell outa you.'

Phil Breen had by now managed to get control

of the shotgun. He waved it at Preacher Scrubbs.

'You may not have been stealin' it,' he said, 'but you sure as hell didn't aim to pay no rental on it.'

Old Fred grinned as he listened to the row. He kept thinking of the jug of whiskey that he had spirited out of the canyon.

'I intended no such thing,' the preacher protested huffily. 'I just needed the animal and had no wish to disturb you so late at night. We could have settled the score in the morning.'

Marshal Cassidy heaved a sigh. He should have been in bed alongside his buxom young wife, and here was all this fuss that could last until dawn. He rapped on the desk with his knuckles and brought about a sudden silence.

All eyes turned on him as he surveyed the office. Ma Breen and her husband still wore their night-clothes under some outer garments. The stout livery man breathed beer fumes every time he opened his mouth while his wife's grey hair, done up in curling wires, had come loose in places and was hanging over her eyes.

The preacher and Fred, both wet and tired, dripped water on the floor, and only the marshal and the mayor presented normal appearances. Luke Cassidy was a young man, recently wed, with a long, thin face and prominent brows. His eyes were a startling blue and held a hint of humour, even at this hour of the morning. He tried to sum up the problem so that they could all get back to bed.

'So you found a wagon loaded with goods up in Dead Man's Canyon,' he said quietly, 'and decided it would be a good idea to bring it back to town before anybody stole it. Is that right, Preacher?'

'That is correct. Fred and I felt we were doin' the work of the Lord by bein' good neighbours to some unfortunate soul.'

'What's in the wagon?' It was Mayor Kroner who barked the question.

There was a long silence and Fred's grin grew wider as he watched the workings of the preacher's gaunt face.

'You did look, didn't you?' the marshal prompted.

'We sure did.' Fred chuckled.

'And?'

'Whiskey,' the preacher said in a small voice.

'How much whiskey?'

'One hell of a lot, Marshal,' Fred said before the preacher could get a word in. 'And some brandy.'

'I can see why you'd want to get it back to town,' Mayor Kroner said with a slight smile. 'What sort of value would we be talkin' about?'

Fred shrugged. 'Hundreds of dollars, Mayor. The town could stay drunk for a year.'

Phil Breen's dull eyes lightened up at the prospect but a glare from his wife kept him silent. The marshal stood up in a decisive attempt to end the meeting.

'Well, I'll tell you what we'll do,' he said firmly. 'I'll take a draught-animal out there first thing in

17

the mornin' and we'll bring the wagon back to town. The whiskey can be stored here in the jail-house until somebody claims it.'

'And if it isn't claimed?' the preacher asked eagerly.

'That's up to Judge Mason.'

Obadiah Scrubb's face fell, but it was Fred who spoke up.

'I reckon as how we shouldn't wait till morning, Marshal,' he urged. 'It could vanish by then, and Judge Mason would be real sore at leavin' such valuable stuff out in that canyon all night.'

'I'll rent you old Bess,' Phil Breen put in.

Luke Cassidy hesitated. He looked out of the window at the row of faces that were peering in and at the rain that fell steadily out of the dark sky. He glanced at the one man in the room who had authority. Mayor Kroner was a stolid, lantern-jawed man with a craggy face that showed determination and strength.

'I think you'd better go, Luke,' he said in his gravelly voice. 'If it's legal, we gotta protect it, and if it's stolen, we gotta recover it. Either way, that whiskey wagon has to come into town. Judge Mason could cut up mighty rough if it didn't.'

'I guess you're right, Mayor,' the marshal agreed reluctantly. 'But I'll need someone with me to help hitch up the horse. How about you, Phil?'

The livery man blinked and threw a glance at his wife.

'Is you paying?' he asked.

The mayor sighed. 'We're paying, Phil. Usual rates.'

'I get extra for workin' nights and in this weather.'

The next ten minutes were spent arguing, and at the end of it all, Obadiah retired to his bed a disappointed man. Fred had long since left the office while the marshal and Phil Breen got ready to brave the elements. The townsfolk gradually dispersed and Huyton went to sleep again.

The rain stopped as suddenly as it had started. There was still lightning on the horizon and a distant growl of thunder. Phil Breen rode the draught-horse with just a blanket for a saddle. Luke Cassidy was astride his bay mare, his lithe body covered with a long oilskin coat. They travelled for the most part in silence.

Dead Man's Canyon was a ride of nearly two hours at the best of times, but in darkness and with the ground slippery, it took them even longer to reach the sloping walls that dipped between the two buttes to make the gash that had once been a river coming down from distant hills.

The clouds were parting when they reached it and a cold wind blew from the north. The moon took a glimpse and threw shadows on the ground which made the going even more deceptive for the horses. Their hoofs echoed between the walls of greyish stone as the two men moved slowly up to where the long line of cholla still creaked in the wind that blew down the canyon.

There was no wagon.

Luke Cassidy got down from his mount and went over to inspect the ground. Phil Breen watched for a moment before getting down from his own horse and going to join him.

'We're wastin' our time,' he said. 'Them two saw somethin' else and got the wrong idea. Or maybe Fred was drinkin' again and the preacher joined him.'

'No, there was a wagon.'

Luke pointed to the deep ruts that still oozed water. There were also fresh horse-droppings and some of the cholla was damaged where the wagon had passed it to head north up the canyon.

'Then I reckon that whoever owned it has come back with a fresh horse and taken his whiskey.' Phil snorted. 'And remember, Marshal, you still owes me, whiskey or no whiskey. They ain't headin' for town, that's one thing sure.'

The lawman looked around carefully.

'They couldn't turn a wagon in this space,' he agreed slowly, 'so they'd have to head north and then move west and south again. Unless they was goin' Fort Rushton way. Let's do a little trailing.'

Phil Breen let out a groan and reluctantly followed the lawman back to where their mounts waited patiently.

They rode up the canyon until reaching the far end where the hills could be seen as black silhouettes against the moon. The ground ahead was a series of little valleys gradually rising to meet the foothills with their lessening tree-growth. Luke turned west, following a line of newly made ruts in the wet ground. There was a stronger light now as the clouds cleared the moon completely and let it shine with a brilliant hardness that faded the stars close to it. Luke Cassidy could follow the trail easily in the wet ground.

'There they are!'

It was Phil Breen who saw the moving shapes head. Luke sighted them too; a covered wagon, white against the dark background, and another figure close by on horseback. The two men speeded up their mounts, the marshal with a certain eagerness, and Phil reluctantly as he tried to stay on the back of the unsaddled horse.

Luke could make out the driver on the wagon and the horseman who rode to the right of it. The distance was about half a mile or so and the rig was moving towards a broad band of trees that would soon hide it from view. The lawman wanted to catch up with them, partly to satisfy his curiosity, but also to make sure that the wagon was not being stolen under his nose.

The shot took him by surprise. It echoed through the night air and passed harmlessly somewhere over his left shoulder. Phil Breen let out a yell and yanked furiously at the reins of his mount. Luke Cassidy pressed on. He spurred his mare as she moved over the rough ground as fast as conditions allowed. Another shot came at him. He could see the tiny flash spurt from the barrel of a gun in the distance. The range was too great for a rider to hope to hit anything, but the men with the wagon were determined to warn off their pursuers.

He galloped furiously, calling on Phil to follow as the wagon speeded up. Another shot flew out of the darkness. The marshal could move faster over the ground than the driver of the wagon, and was soon gaining on it. He drew his own Colt .44 and fired a warning shot.

It had occured to him that they might think he and Phil were trying to steal their load of whiskey, and as he got nearer, Luke shouted out his name and waved the gun in the air to let them know that he was a lawman.

If he hoped it would bring the wagon to a halt, he was mistaken. Both the fleeing men fired at him again and the bullets flew closer as the range shortened. He knew that they must have heard him, and decided to try a trick that might be more effective. He stopped his mount, slipped the Winchester from its saddle holster, and took careful aim from a stationary position. The horse drawing the wagon stumbled in its tracks, recovered for a moment, and slowed down noticeably.

'We've got 'em, Phil!' the marshal shouted exultantly as he levered another cartridge into position and put spurs to his horse.

The driver of the wagon had pulled on the reins and brought it to a halt. He scrambled down and, after taking another shot at the approaching lawman, jumped up behind the other rider. The pair set off towards the line of trees and quickly disappeared from sight.

By the time Luke Cassidy reached the rig, the two men had been swallowed in the darkness of the wooded area. There was no chance of catching up with them and he had to be content with recovering the load of liquor. The horse was now on its knees, breathing heavily and making slight gurgling noises. Luke examined the wound, shook his head sadly, and put a bullet in the animal's head.

It was only at this point that he realized that Phil Breen was not with him. In all the excitement, he had taken it for granted that the man had been just behind him. But the livery stable did not apparently breed heroes. Phil was riding his horse very slowly about sixty yards away. He approached carefully and got down from the large draught-animal.

'That was a good bit of work, Marshal,' he said carefully. 'I reckon as how you'll be needin' my help now.'

'I could have used a bit of backin' when them fellas was shootin' at me,' Luke said contemptuously.

'Oh, I'm no gunslinger,' Phil admitted happily. 'Don't even carry a gun, Marshal, and you ain't deputized me as no posse fella. I just supply old Bess here and you does the rest.'

'That figures. Right, then let's you and me get

the shafts off the dead horse and back the wagon a few yards. Then we'll hitch your animal and take this lot back to town.'

It was hard work. Both men were strongly muscled but it took the two men half an hour to untangle the mess and attach old Bess to the shafts of the little rig. Phil had glanced inside and seen the load of whiskey and brandy. His mouth was virtually watering by the time he climbed up on the box and took the reins in his hands.

Dawn was breaking when they set off to travel back to Huyton township. A thin mist lay over the ground and water still oozed out of the wet soil as they moved back through the canyon and headed due south. Luke rode at the side of the wagon, letting his mare pick her own way across the ground. He leaned over in the saddle to speak to Phil.

'That horse back there,' he said in a casual voice. 'Did you ever see it before?'

The liveryman turned in his seat and considered the matter carefully.

'Can't say that I have,' he said after a moment's thought. 'There was no brand and it was quite an old animal. The shoes were in good condition and it was well fed. I reckon it was a saddle-horse more than a draught animal. Didn't have the usual harness marks.'

Luke nodded. 'Could have come from anywhere,' he said. 'Pity they got away.'

Phil looked dubious. 'Maybe it was for the best,

Marshal,' he suggested. 'You was only one gun, and them two fellas could have outshot you if they'd not lost one horse and gotten into a panic.'

'They made a run for it because you were behind me, Phil,' Luke said with a slight grin. 'They thought as how you was backin' me.'

The liveryman chuckled. 'Well, they was sure wrong there, fella. I was all ready to turn tail and head for home.'

They travelled for another mile or so, with the noise of waking birds competing against the clatter of the wagon. Phil was wide awake and confident now. He was already working on a story he could tell in the saloon about how he had helped the marshal outgun the thieves. If he played things the right way, there would be plenty of free drinks.

The sudden tap on the shoulder came as a nasty surprise and he let out a frightened yell as he turned to look at the face that peered at him from between the canvas covers of the wagon.

THREE

Old Fred Brown had good reason to leave the marshal's office while they were still arguing about going out to the canyon. He was concocting a little plan of his own. He hurried back to the cabin where he lived with a mangy dog and an elderly mule, and tucked away the stolen jug of whiskey under his bed.

Then he saddled the mule and set off for Dead Man's Canyon at as good a speed as the animal could muster. There was still plenty of time to get there before the marshal and Phil Breen. He could snaffle a few more jugs of liquor and be away before they got to the scene. Old Fred's lips slavered as he dug his heels into the flanks of the animal and headed north through the night.

He had been careful to keep well off the main street and nobody saw him leave town. For all his superstitious fear of the canyon, the promise of free whiskey was too much to resist.

The old man was sweating and breathing heavily by the time his goal was reached. He was also feeling the effects of the alcohol he had already drunk and was too muddled to tie the animal properly to the back of the wagon. The rein slipped as Fred climbed up over the tailboard to luxuriate among the precious cargo.

He took four stone jars and placed them ready to strap across his saddle. As he bent to gather up some more, it occured to him that a small drink might quieten his heavy heartbeat. He opened one of the jars and took a large pull. It did not do much for his heart rhythm but he felt distinctly better and took another swig.

It was quite an effort to get down from the wagon and tie the four jugs across the cantle. He stood rubbing his chin before deciding that a couple more flasks could be carried as well. He climbed back on board and stumbled over a case of brandy. Fred peered at the fancy labels on the bottles as he removed a couple from the thick bedding of straw. They could hardly be seen in the dark, but he had never tasted brandy and now was the time to try it. He broke the neck of one of the bottles against a barrel and sampled the contents.

His long sigh of pleasure was audible to the mule as it looked around for something to eat. Finding nothing interesting, and with its reins hanging free, it decided to go home and trotted happily out of the canyon.

Fred never noticed. He was sitting amid the boxes and jars, cosy and snug against the night air.

The bottle of brandy was clutched in his hand and he sipped away gently until he fell asleep.

He was not quite sure what woke him. The wagon was shaking a little, and some of the stone jars were clattering against each other. He sat with his back to a wooden crate of whiskey and tried to focus his eyes on the dark interior.

There were voices, and he could hear the jingle of harness as a horse was pushed into the shafts. Fred wanted to get to his feet and peer out of the wagon to see what was happening. But his feet did not seem to work, while his eyes were watering to blur his vision. He remembered where he was and what was supposed to be happening.

Marshal Cassidy had arrived with help to move the load of drink back to town. Fred relaxed again. It was too late for him to beat a retreat with his stolen liquor, but he could at least sit tight and let them take him home again. He wondered vaguely whether or not they had seen his mule. If they had, they might open the canvas flaps and discover him amid the bottles and jars. He grinned owlishly and snuggled down out of sight.

The jolting woke him up again. The rig was moving fast and he was being thrown about as it creaked and the cargo shifted around. Old Fred tried to hang on to the half-empty bottle that was resting on his lap. If it flew out of his hand and went rattling along the boards, the noise might alert Marshal Cassidy and whoever was with him to his presence. He clung frantically to one of the large crates as he bounced up and down. He could make out very little in the dark interior of the wagon, but his acute hearing could pick out the brushing of cactus against the vehicle and the cursing of the driver up on the box. The rig bumped violently over some rocks, splitting some of the planks that floored it. Fred's arm slipped down the widening crack and he withdrew it hurriedly from among the splintered edges.

The shot seemed to be almost behind his head and he jumped at the sudden noise. A second shot split the air and the old man threw himself as flat as he could on the damaged flooring. His hands covered his sweaty face as the rig speeded up and two large flasks shattered as they struck each other and flooded the place with whiskey. It was seeping all over Fred but he had lost interest in it.

Another shot echoed around him but it seemed to be some distance away and was not as frightening until he looked up and saw that there was a tear in the canvas above him. He could see the lightening sky with a solitary star peeping at him through the scurrying clouds.

The wagon travelled on for a while until another distant shot tore through the night. The rig suddenly slowed down, then got up speed again before almost stopping. Fred could hear the driver cursing as he climbed down from the wagon and left it standing in a sudden silence. The old man could hear horses moving around and decided to lie low. He picked up the fallen bottle, saw that it was empty and decided to open another. He needed something to calm his nerves.

Fred took a long swig from the bottle and settled against a crate that seemed like some feather pillow to his ageing back. He looked up at the rent in the canvas, vaguely heard some more movement, and then drifted off to sleep.

That was why Phil Breen let out such a yell and nearly fell off the wagon.

The last thing he was expecting was a tap on the shoulder and an unshaven face thrust at him in the dawning light. Poor Fred received a hearty push, and was left to console himself with a few more drinks that compensated for the verbal abuse as they headed back for town.

'Did you see who they were?'

That was the first question that Marshal Cassidy asked when they sat in the warmth of his office with large mugs of coffee in front of them.

'Just fellas, is all,' Fred replied sleepily. 'I didn't see nothing, Marshal. Can I go home now?'

The lawman nodded. 'You may as well, but if you think of any way we can check on them fellas, let me know.'

'I'll do that, Marshal,' the old man said thankfully as he scurried out of the office to weave his way uncertainly to the shack. His mule was safely by the corral with the dog for company. The jars still hung from the cantle and Fred's eyes filled with tears at the prospects that lay before him.

After watching the old drunk wander off, Luke Cassidy turned to the tired liveryman.

'Well, Phil,' he said cheerfully, 'I reckon as how you and me has to move all that liquor into one of the cells. So drink up and let's get to it.'

Old Fred sat on the edge of his narrow bed in the flickering candlelight. He was drunk and tired, but not as drunk or tired as the others had believed. He had to stay awake to work out a few things. Dawn was already up over the distant hills and light was coming through the dirty window to brighten up the squalid little cabin in which he lived.

He drank some more of the strong coffee that bubbled on the stove, and finally made up his mind. He rose shakily from the bed and fumbled his way to an old chest on which lay a heap of dirty clothes and a pair of worn boots. He brushed them on to the earthen floor and threw open the lid of the wooden box.

After a little fishing around, he drew forth an old Navy Colt, a bullet-mould, some pieces of lead, and a ladle. A little more searching produced a box of percussion caps and a copper powder horn. Fred started making preparations to arm himself.

He was quite sober by the time he reached his destination. It was broad daylight by now and people were moving about on the main street. Fred kept out of sight, using the back lanes and heading purposefully for the rear door of a particular building.

He tapped on it gently after peering in through the window to make sure that his quarry was there. The door opened and the old man leered as he braced himself for a confrontation.

'I got me some news,' he said huskily. 'And I reckon as how it's worth the price of a few drinks.'

'You've already had a few drinks by the look of it, Fred. Go home and sleep it off.'

'Oh, I've swallowed a few this last hour or so, but I ain't so drunk as I don't know what I saw and heard.'

The person who had opened the door looked carefully up and down the rutted lane.

'You'd better come inside then.'

Fred placed a hand on the butt of the old Colt and entered the building.

FOUR

Marshal Luke Cassidy stood at the door of the open cell and waited patiently while Mosher Davis ran his experienced eye over the collection of whiskey and brandy that occupied the space intended for law-breakers.

Mosher was a large, muscled man of about fifty, with a sad face and a drooping moustache that hid the tight creases around his ruthless mouth. His piggy eyes were half-closed as he calculated the value of the haul found in the canyon. He whistled gently to himself as he reckoned up the totals. His dark waistcoat and black stock were spattered with cigar ash as were the lapels of his cut-away coat. He turned at last to the marshal with his verdict.

'Well, Luke,' he said in solemn tones, 'I reckon as how there's the best part of three hundred dollarsworth of liquor in this here cell. I ain't seen such high-falutin' stuff outside Phoenix. It's a real class haul, let me tell you, and somebody is surely in mournin' for its loss.'

'Any ideas, Mosher?'

The saloon-owner shrugged.

'Not really,' he admitted, 'but it had to be stolen from somewhere to end up in that canyon. Didn't nobody see the fellas who tried to take it?'

'We saw them, but at a distance. They got clear away and all we was left with was old Fred. Drunk as a skunk.'

Mosher managed a very rare smile.

'So I heard tell,' he said. 'And that reminds me, I ain't seen him around these last two days. He's usually in my place as soon as he's earned a few cents.'

Mosher's place was the only saloon in town. It was rather optimistically called the Golden Chance and had made Mosher Davis a pretty wealthy man. This was reflected in his gold watch-chain, signet rings, and large diamond pin in his stock. He moved in an aura of Cologne and cigars and was a pillar of the local community.

'I think he made off with one or two jars of this stuff,' Luke explained. 'He'll probably be drunk for a week or so. Well, we'll just have to wait for somethin' to happen. It's at times like these when I wish we had the telegraph. Maybe the stage will bring some news.'

Mosher Davis turned a sly look on the young marshal.

'And suppose there ain't no claimant,' he said slowly, 'what then?'

Luke Cassidy shrugged.

'I reckon as how the judge will have to give an

34

opinion on that, Mosher.'

'It would have to be sold off,' the saloon keeper mused. 'I would be interested if the price was right.'

'You said about three hundred dollars.'

Mosher shook his head sadly. 'Three hundred if the stuff was being sold across a bar,' he explained as to a backward child. 'And some of this stuff is too fancy for a town like Huyton. No, I'd be willing to go to perhaps one hundred. With a bonus of twenty dollars for the man who put the deal through.'

He looked hard at the lawman as he spoke.

'It'll all rest with the judge,' Luke Cassidy said flatly.

'Only you and me knows the value,' Mosher suggested, 'and twenty dollars is as much as any town marshal earns in a week.'

Luke Cassidy took the big man by the elbow and propelled him out of the cell. He slammed the door shut and turned the key.

'Just listen good and loud, fella,' he said menacingly. 'You try bribin' me and you'll be in the next cell to that lot of liquor.'

Mosher dragged his arm away angrily and slid a large hand beneath his coat. Before he could pull the gun that was hidden there, Luke Cassidy had drawn his own .44 and the barrel was digging into the man's ample waistline.

'You'd better leave while you still can,' he said grimly.

'I pull me some weight in this town,' Mosher

snarled. 'You're pickin' a quarrel with the wrong man.'

Luke Cassidy pushed the saloon-keeper back against the wall of the office.

'I got me an idea about all this business,' he said quietly. 'I figure as how some smart fella bought a load of stolen liquor and it was left in Dead Man's Canyon to be collected from town and brought in quietly durin' the night. Obadiah and Fred upset them plans and when word went around town about it, somebody high-tailed it to the canyon to move the stuff before we got there. Now, maybe I'm wrong, but the man with the money for all this and the man with the means to sell it, is right at the end of this gun. What do you think, Mosher?'

The saloon-keeper's face was a dull red and sweat poured down into his eyes.

'You're talkin' like a young fool,' he snarled. 'I don't need to trade like that. I got me a reputation, and I aim to be mayor when Ned Kroner steals enough to retire or that fat wife of his rolls over and smothers him. You've known me for years, Luke Cassidy. I may try and pull off a deal, but do you really believe what you're saying?'

'Let's see if we can prove you ain't the fella then. You've got a horse that pulls your surrey, Mosher. Let's go take a look at it.'

'Sure. Why not?'

The saloon-keeper headed for the door, but not before the lawman reached under Mosher's coat and removed the short-barrelled gun that lay concealed there. They left the jailhouse and walked along the street, past the saloon, and down a side lane where Mosher Davis kept his riding-horse and carriage-horse in a small corral. Both animals were there and looked across the rails in curiosity as the two men came in sight.

Luke handed the gun back.

'Satisfied?' Mosher asked sarcastically.

'I reckon so. The animal pullin' that wagon was one without a brand, and I ain't had anyone tell me they knows who owns it. Seen Wes Brendel lately?'

The saloon keeper bridled angrily.

'Don't throw that up at me,' he snarled. 'I got rid of that no-good low-life when he shot up the town last year.'

'Some folks say as how you still use him to collect debts and settle with drunks.'

The man shrugged.

'He does odd jobs,' he admitted. 'Nothin' more. I don't keep him around full time. He's too quick to make trouble.'

Mosher stood hesitatingly for a moment. One hand was stroking the head of his riding-animal as he looked at the marshal with calculating eyes.

'I got me an enemy in this town,' he said quietly. 'I ain't sayin' as how he wants me dead or anythin' like that, but he sure as hell wants my business.'

'You're talkin' about Bill Harley?'

Mosher nodded with sudden eagerness.

'Yes, he's tryin' to build that hotel of his into a

gamblin' place and saloon. He gets all the travellers from the stage, and reckons that to have a saloon and a few card-tables would really pay off big.'

Marshal Cassidy thought about it for a moment.

'And you figure that Bill Harley is behind all this?' he asked.

'Who else? Just think about it, Luke. He has the money and the ambition.'

The marshal nodded non-committally and walked slowly away. As he moved down the main street, he saw the man they had been talking about. He was speaking to a neighbour just outside the Harley House hotel. The lawman crossed over and waited until the conversation broke up.

Bill Harley was a tall, thin man, of just about equal height to Luke but with a gaunt face and bushy eyebrows that met above his nose. He dressed neatly but without the showiness of the saloon-owner, and greeted the lawman with a slight smile.

'I saw you goin' round to the corrals with Mosher,' he said quietly. 'Did he put a valuation on the liquor?'

Luke grinned. 'He sure did. A real low one at that.'

'I thought he might, but as I told you yesterday, that stuff is worth at least five hundred dollars and nobody in this town would touch it. Too fancy by half.'

Luke Cassidy leaned against the hitching rail.

'Tell me, Bill,' he probed, 'could a man get a better class of trade by sellin' that sort of liquor?'

'You mean me?' The hotel-keeper laughed to show his yellowing teeth. 'I don't get enough folk in my place, and I can't make it more like a saloon or I'll lose the travellin' trade. Folks like a quiet hotel.'

'And what about Mosher?'

Bill Harley shrugged.

'I'd like to put it down to him, but I don't see as how I can. He don't serve real whiskey in the Golden Chance. He uses high wines, as they're called in the trade. Dilutes the stuff half-and-half with water. Then as the night goes on, he adds more water. It's all part of the saloon trade. That stuff you've got would be wasted on his customers.'

Luke Cassidy glanced vaguely up and down the near-deserted street. He was trying to spot a familiar figure.

'Seen anythin' of old Fred?' he asked the hotel-owner.

'Not for a few days, but I hear tell that he got some of the whiskey tucked away while the goin' was good. He won't be back in the land of the livin' until it's all gone, I reckon. Why not ask the preacher? Fred usually works for him when he's sober enough.'

'He's not seen him. What about Wes Brendel?'

The hotel-keeper pulled a face.

'Proppin' up Mosher's bar, I shouldn't wonder.

That, or startin' a fight somewhere. It's all he's good for.'

'No, he seems to have vanished like old Fred. See you around, Bill.'

The marshal walked slowly back to his office and stood uncertainly on the stoop for a few minutes. He decided to pay a visit to old Fred's cabin. It was tucked away behind the main street, in a small lane that lay between the schoolhouse and the corral where the teacher and the bank president kept their animals.

It was a dismal place that he had never visited before. The plank door hung on two leather hinges and sagged at the wooden latch. There were pieces of worn sacking over the two broken windows, and the iron pipe of a stove poked out of one corner of the wall where some stone had been built in to take the heat. There was no smoke from the stove and the whole place appeared deserted.

He recalled vaguely that Fred had a mule and a mangy, starved-looking dog that barked at everyone who passed. There was no sign of either of them.

He banged on the door with his fist, not expecting an answer, and not getting one. The latch lifted easily but he had to raise the door to let it pass over the rough ground that made up the floor of the cabin. A wave of fetid hot air hit him as he entered the darkness.

As the marshal's eyes grew accustomed to the dimness of the little place, he could make out the bed, a rough table, and the old chest where Fred kept his treasures. A few roaches scuttled across the floor as the lawman crossed to one of the windows and pulled the sacking aside. He looked round in the better light and saw what had interested the insects. There was dried blood on the bed and mixed with the dirt on the floor.

FIVE

Thursday was the big day for the folks of Huyton. The stage arrived with all the news from the cities, and if the little place was lucky, a few travellers might stay over in the comfort of the Harley House hotel to bring the gossip of a wider world.

Luke Cassidy waited anxiously. The stage was later than usual. It normally pulled up in a flurry of dust some time before noon, but it was now nearly four and still no sign of it. The trail was bad after heavy rain, and there had been mud-slides in several places. The marshal hoped that it was nothing more than that. He sat in his office, drinking coffee and listening for the sound of wheels and horses.

It was close on five of the clock before the stage pulled up in front of the Wells Fargo depot and began unloading its freight. Luke Cassidy hurried along the street to wait impatiently while the few passengers alighted and their luggage was passed down. He edged round the fussy little clerk and grabbed the driver by the arm.

'Anythin' wrong, Bert?' he asked anxiously.

The man turned to see who was interrupting his talk with the clerk. His face cleared when he recognized the marshal.

'I was just comin' to see you, Luke,' he said thankfully. 'We had a bit of trouble up near Malvern Greek. There's a burnt-out wagon there and a dead body. Been around a few days, I'd reckon, and the fella is too badly burnt to hang a name on.'

'Any sign of a fight?'

The man shrugged.

'I'm no law-enforcin' fella,' he said uncertainly, 'but there ain't no horse around, and somebody had to turn it loose. We searched the area in case there was anybody lyin' wounded in the mesquite. There weren't nothin' we could find so we gave up and got into town before dark. I couldn't risk drivin' a four-up rig without daylight.'

Luke thanked the man for his information, collected the latest Tombstone newspapers, and walked slowly back to his office. There was nothing he could do until daylight, and so decided to read through the journals in case there was any report of stolen liquor, and then discuss the affair with the mayor first thing in the morning.

Screwing up his eyes to read the small print in the feeble lamplight, he scanned the *Tombstone Nugget* and the *Tombstone Epitaph* without success. There was no mention of any robbery of whiskey or brandy. A gun-store had been raided; there had been a shoot-out in one of the saloons, but most of the stories were of politicians dipping their hands into public funds. He put the papers away and decided to call it a night.

The morning was clear with a slight wind that brought the reddish dust to rise in tight swirls. Luke left town early, after a talk with the mayor. He travelled at a brisk pace, covering the distance to the creek in under an hour. The local mortician was at his side, riding a large mule and followed by a cart bearing a wooden casket and driven by his young assistant.

The area they were heading for was like a little oasis in an otherwise dull landscape of scrub and tall cacti. The creek lay in a slight fold of sandstone ridges and came up clear and fast-moving, to disappear again beneath overhanging rock. Lush growth prospered around it and small creatures scattered at the noise of the marshal's little procession.

A slight smell in the air was enough to let Luke Cassidy know, even before they reached the spot, that something had been burning. The remains of the wagon lay upon the charred ground, the metal parts standing out like ribs among the blackened timbers. A collection of smaller ribs shone amid the wreckage. They were human remains which had been burned beyond recognition and then picked at by every local predator.

The three men stood looking at the mess while

their animals quietly munched at the rich grass.

'Sure was one hell of a fire,' the mortician's young assistant murmured as he scratched his head in wonderment.

The marshal did not answer. He had spotted something and bent over the pile of crumbling wood to pick up the blackened pistol that lay near the body. It was an old Colt Navy model, damaged by the explosions of the charges and with the wooden butt burned away.

'Old Fred,' he said sadly. 'I reckon he came out here for some reason, and was so drunk that he accidentally set the rig alight.'

'So where's the horse?' the mortician asked. He was a tall, thin man with a face as miserable as that of Preacher Scrubbs.

It was a good question and Luke Cassidy recalled the stage-driver saying that somebody had to unharness the animal. He stood uncertainly as he looked around in some sort of vain hope that a loose horse might be close by amid the rich pasture and ample supply of water.

'Well, I figure as how we have a real mystery here,' he said despondently. 'We don't even know where Fred got hold of a horse and wagon.'

'Could have been doin' a cartin' job for some-body,' the mortician suggested.

'Could be. We'll have to ask around town.' Luke nodded towards the body. 'Anyhows, let's get this back and have the preacher do a burial.'

The young assistant went to the little cart and

hauled off the cheap wooden casket. He placed it near the wreckage and laid the lid next to it to await the orders of his boss. His face was a study in puzzlement and he could not resist saying what he felt.

'It takes one hell of a lot to set a rig like this on fire,' he said in a tentative way. 'How could it be done?'

That was the very question that the marshal had been asking himself. It was one he hated to acknowledge. He just shook his head and watched as the two men tried to remove the body without its falling apart. Luke Cassidy walked slowly round the burnt-out wagon while they were working. It was no use looking for marks on the trail. Too many hoofs and wheels had passed by. He was wondering what had been carried on the rig and what had caused the fire. Old Fred smoked a pipe when he had money to buy tobacco, but the marshal could not figure any way in which dropped ash could cause such a conflagration. There was also a smell about the wreck. It was lamp-oil.

'I reckon Doc Hibbert should take a look at the body when we get to town,' he said as he walked back to his horse and took up the reins. 'I'd like to know how he died.'

The mortician gave a slight grimace that might have been an attempt at a grin.

'I can't tell you that,' he said, 'but the ribs are smashed clean through to the spine.'

Luke nodded. 'Sounds like a shooting. But why?'

The mortician shrugged and moved a little closer to the marshal.

'Maybe the fella who's watchin' us might know the answer to that,' he suggested.

Luke Cassidy's right hand slipped down to the comforting feel of the gun at his side. He was furious with himself for not having spotted the watcher before the mortician did.

'Where is he?' he asked tersely.

'Just behind that clump of mesquite. Turned up while you were lookin' at the rig.'

Luke reached out for the saddle holster that contained his Winchester. He drew the weapon swiftly, turning towards the mesquite as he cocked it. He fired a shot above the clump. There was a yell of fright and the mesquite trembled amid a shower of dust as a horseman fought to control his animal. Luke waited patiently while the mortician and his assistant watched with a certain detached interest.

'I ain't doin' no harm, Marshal!' a voice shouted hoarsely. 'I ain't even armed.'

'Come outa there, Phil,' the lawman ordered. He had already identified the voice and lowered the gun while Phil Breen steered his startled animal round the clump of bushes and into the open.

'What in hell was you skulkin' there for!' Luke asked angrily. 'You could have had your head blowed off'n your shoulders.'

'I had to be sure it was you, Marshal,' the man answered as he dismounted. 'I came with a message from town. We got trouble back there.'

Luke Cassidy sighed heavily.

'What's happenin' that's so bad I gotta be chased out here?' he asked.

'It's that hotel fella and Mosher Davis. They're threatenin' to shoot each other over that load of whiskey we brought into town. Mosher reckons as how the hotel fella is tryin' to steal his trade and set up another saloon.'

'Well, I don't figure as how I can do much,' the lawman said quietly. 'It musta taken you an hour or so to get here, and it'll take me that time to get back again. It should all be over by the time we arrive on the scene.'

He turned to the mortician with a wide grin.

'Sounds more like your sorta business, Harry,' he said.

The mortician nodded happily at the thought of a burial for one or even two of the richest men in Huyton.

'Perhaps we ought to get going,' he suggested as he gestured to his assistant to mount the wagon.

Luke glanced at the livery man who was now on foot and examining the burnt-out rig. The man seemed anxious as he peered at the wreckage.

'Lookin' for something, Phil?' he asked gently.

The livery man jumped back a couple of feet.

'No, nothin' in particular, Marshal,' he

protested. 'Just wonderin' where the horse is.'

'Yeah, I've been wonderin' about that. Ever seen the wagon before?'

Phil Breen shook his head vigorously.

'Can't say as I have, Marshal,' he said with emphasis.

Luke grinned. 'Well, I think I have. It brought a load of whiskey into town and was stored behind your livery stable. You sure got a lotta questions to answer, fella.'

SIX

The marshal's office was hot under the light of the oil-lamps. Luke Cassidy sat at his desk and faced a livery-stable owner who sweated in the closeness of the room. A solitary moth fluttered around one of the lamps, making the only noise as the two men stared at each other.

'Now, let's get this straight, Phil,' the marshal said patiently. 'Two days ago you rented out the rig and a horse to Wes Brendel. Is that right?'

The man nodded eager agreement.

'Sure is, Marshal,' he stuttered. 'He said that he had some furniture to move for old Ma Wesley. Paid a good price he did, and never argued the toss.'

'Phil, it wasn't your wagon.'

'Well – no, but it was only to be out for a day or two, and I reckon there weren't no reason to have it standin' idle, gatherin' dust.'

'And this tale you told me about Mosher and Bill Harley gunnin' for each other. That was just to

50

explain what you was doin' out at the creek?'

The man nodded glumly.

'I guess so,' he admitted. 'I wanted to see if it was my rig what got burned up. Besides, it weren't a lie, Marshal. They was bad-mouthin' each other earlier in the day. Met on the street, they did, and Mosher comes straight out with it. Says that the hotel fella is tryin' to steal his trade. Threatened him, he did.'

Luke stood up and crossed to open the office door.

'I guess you'd better get off home, Phil,' he said. 'And you'd best think up some good story in case the owner of that rig comes into town. If he's totin' a gun, we might be lookin' for a new fella to run the livery stable.'

'It ain't my fault, Marshal,' the man whined, 'and I lost me a good horse out there.'

'Your horse might come home in a day or two, but that's more than old Fred Brown will. One more thing. Was he with Wes Brendel when you did the deal?'

'No. Ain't seen Fred since the night the whiskey wagon arrived, in town.'

'Sleep well, Phil.'

Luke watched the man until he was out of sight at the other end of the main street. Then he checked his pocket-watch and decided to go across to the Golden Chance, where the mayor was likely to be enthroned in his nightly pose as the solid pillar of the community. Some official report would have to be made and the saloon was a more congenial place for composing it than the confines of the mayoral office behind a dry-goods store.

Mayor Kroner was leaning on the bar of the smoky and noisy room. His sturdy figure and massive jaw dominated the scene as much as his loud voice and the fact that he bought drinks for everybody who approached him. It was a reminder to the lawman that an election was due in a few months' time. Lawyer Gravitt and the saloon-owner were both anxious to supplant their old rival.

Gravitt was at the other end of the bar, his solemn face a mask of contempt for the open-handedness of the mayoral court. It looked like being an interesting election.

Luke went to join the mayor, accepted a drink and told him what had happened. The First Citizen nodded sadly as though he felt some genuine emotion for the death of old Fred.

'So what do you reckon happened out there?' he asked.

It was the question that Luke Cassidy had been trying to answer all evening.

'Well,' he said slowly, 'I figure that Wes Brendel needed a wagon for some reason we ain't fathomed yet. And he needed someone to help him shift whatever load he had in mind. So he hired old Fred. A dollar and a few drinks would do that easy enough. Then they had a fallin' out and Wes shot the old fella and burned the rig to cover it up.'

'And what happened to Wes?'

'He lit out on the horse, maybe. Sure as hell would put some distance between himself and this town. I still can't figure why the wagon burned so easily, though. Some brandy was spilt the night we brought it in, but I doubt if that would have done it. I felt that I could smell lamp-oil out there.'

'Maybe that's what they was carrying,' the mayor said with sudden inspiration. 'Wes Brendel will be no loss, but – old Fred. He was harmless.'

'Yeah, folks will be mighty riled when they hear what happened to him. I'm also told that our two richest citizens are on the prod with each other.'

The mayor snorted.

'They had a real stand-up row on the main street earlier today,' he said. 'Could have ended in a shoot-out if Doc Hibbert hadn't parted them. Seems that Mosher is set on thinkin' that the load of liquor was comin' into town to ruin his trade.'

Luke grimaced. 'Ain't likely, but I'd better keep an eye on the two of them.'

He raised the glass to his lips just as the swing-doors of the saloon burst open and a small man with a narrow, anxious face peered around the room. He saw the marshal and hurried across.

'There's two fellas snoopin' round Drugget's gun store, Marshal,' he gasped urgently. 'Tryin' the back door, they was, and seein' if any of the windows was open.'

'Where's Pete Drugget?' the mayor asked, putting his glass down on the bar.

'Him and his wife is at her brother's place, but their kids will be in the building. Young Kate's old enough to look after the other two, but if some fella's tryin' to break in, I reckon she'll be one mighty scared young lady.'

Luke was already on his way out of the saloon. He hurried down the street with the mayor and several other folk trailing well behind him. His Colt .44 was already out of the holster and his thumb covered the hammer ready for use.

Pete Drugget's gun store was quite a small building, built of brick at the front and with sturdy wooden sides and rear. It was well shuttered and no lights showed from the upper windows. The marshal hurried down the narrow passage between it and the neighbouring barbershop. There was little help from the clouded sky and only uncertain glimmers from the main street. He could make out two horses tethered near the gunsmith's corral. He halted to adjust his eyes and ears to the conditions around him.

There was a slight scraping sound from his left and he heard a muffled voice whispering hoarsely. Luke Cassidy was sweating. He needed somebody to go round the other side of the building, but knew his fellow townsmen well enough to realize that there would be few volunteers. He glanced behind him; the little alley was empty. All the local heroes were safely on the main street.

He was not wearing spurs and was able to edge his way along the wall in silence. He poked his head round carefully to get a view of the back door of the building. His informant had been right. Two vague figures were trying to force a shuttered window.

Luke took a deep breath and cocked the gun as he stepped out to confront them.

'Just hold it there, fellas!' he shouted. 'This is the law!'

There was a yell of alarm and a piece of metal clattered to the ground. Both men turned towards him as they went for their guns.

Luke fired at the one nearest to him. The flash lit up the surroundings and he could make out two tall, slim fellows in dark shirts and with unshaven faces.

His bullet took the nearer one high in the shoulder and the man stumbled back against his companion. The other man pushed the staggering body away and fired wildly at the marshal. His shot went wide and he did not try to repeat the attempt. He ran along the back of the building to turn the corner into the next alleyway. The lawman let out a grunt of satisfaction. One man was down and the other was left without a horse. He skirted the writhing body on the ground and ran after the fleeing robber.

There was a sudden burst of firing. Shot after shot split the night air as the marshal halted in his stride. Then a burst of what sounded like united triumphantal applause broke out as the townsfolk gathered round the man they had just gunned down.

The mayor had led them to the top of the alley through which the fleeing bandit was approaching the main street. Faced by only one gun, the locals emptied their pistols into the man. He collapsed in a heap and never moved again. The mayor stood over the corpse with a Colt revolver held proudly in one large hand. He had led the brave fighters and was already offering them free drinks back in the saloon as Luke Cassidy approached.

'I reckon as how we settled it all very nicely, Luke,' the First Citizen said modestly. 'Did you kill the other fella?'

'I wounded him,' the marshal answered quietly, 'and I'm sure glad that folks rallied around.'

'They're all good, worthy citizens,' the mayor said in a loud voice. 'I'm right proud to serve 'em as mayor.'

He looked round the dark street at the eager, flushed faces.

'And I hope to continue doin' so for many years.'

There was a chorus of assent and a general air of celebration that was only broken when Doc Hibbert appeared on the scene, followed by the mortician. The doctor was led round the corner by the marshal to tend to the wounded man, who lay in a pool of dark blood just below the window he had been trying to force. He groaned as the medical man probed his shoulder with a questing hand.

'He ain't bad hurt,' Doc Hibbert said cheerfully. 'Get some fellas to carry him to my office and I'll have that bullet out. Then you can hang him all regular like.'

'Stealin' from stores ain't a hangin' matter,' Luke Cassidy said bleakly.

The doctor chuckled as he stood up and wiped his hands on a large bandanna.

'With Judge Mason on the bench and the sorta juries we get in this town, I figure that anythin' but spittin' on the sidewalk is a hangin' offence. Besides, folk have to have some entertainment.'

The marshal nodded glumly.

'You may be right.'

The doctor's surgery was a warm room, made warmer by four large oil-lamps which gave light to the bullet-extraction and the cleansing of the wound. The patient groaned occasionally but stood most of the pain with reasonable fortitude. Doc Hibbert eventually laid down his scissors and wiped bloody hands on a damp towel.

'Well, I reckon that's my contribution,' he said with quiet satisfaction. 'You can take him off to the jailhouse now and I'll come change the dressings

some time tomorrow. I take it the town's footin'
the bill?'

Luke nodded. He helped the injured man get to
his feet.

'Come on, fella. We gotta tuck you in for the
night.'

The man was young and thin, with sharp
features and keen dark eyes. He looked at the two
men and then shrugged, as if giving up. He
walked quietly across the street where folks where
still clustered together. They talked about what
had happened while young Kate Drugget stood
outside her father's store with a shotgun under
her arm and her two siblings hopping excitedly at
her side.

'What happened to Mike?' the prisoner asked as
he was settled into a cell and the door was locked
on him.

'The townsfolk shot him,' Luke answered. 'If
you had broken into the store, that young girl
would have had you both. She's some tough
customer. She won't let anybody steal from her pa.'

The man came across to the bars angrily.

'We wasn't stealing, Marshal,' he protested.

'Well, you sure as hell had me fooled. You try
breakin' open the shutters with an iron bar, and
you have a shoot-out with a law officer. I reckon
Judge Mason will figure that for stealin' easily
enough.'

'No, Marshal. It weren't like that. We was after
the reward.'

Luke Cassidy tried to hide his surprise.

'And what reward was that?' he asked calmly.

'For the guns.'

The lawman went over to the bars and stared hard at the prisoner.

'I think you'd better explain that, fella,' he said.

'Ain't you got a telegraph in this one-horse town?' the man asked with sudden contempt.

'No, we ain't. And we got no gallows either. We just drop you from the loadin' beam at the grain-store,' snapped Luke. 'Get to the point, fella. I don't figure on listenin' to you all night.'

'Well, it was the robbery in Tombstone. Some fella broke into that big gun-store on Fourth Street and stole a load of real pricey merchandise. There's a five-hundred dollar reward posted.'

Luke Cassidy stared hard at the young man for a moment. He was trying to detect some sign of a hard-luck story or some plea of a misunderstanding. The fellow looked genuine enough as he spoke and was rubbing his injured shoulder as the pain nagged him.

'So why come here?' the marshal asked.

The man answered eagerly.

'I'm Hal Levitt,' he said. 'Me and Mike is cowpokes, and we was havin' a few drinks last Saturday night in Tombstone. And who does we see in the saloon but Wes Brendel. Do you know him, Marshal?'

Luke Cassidy was interested now.

'I know him,' he said.

'Well, there he was, large as life and proppin' up the bar. The gun-store was broke into that very night, and Tombstone was in a real takin' about it. Them guns was somethin' special. All fancy pieces from foreign parts that them rich folks has started usin' to show they're better than the other fellas. The store posted a five-hundred dollar reward right pronto, and me and Mike reckoned we had a start on everybody else.'

'How did you figure that?

The man clung to the bars in a desperate attempt to make his point.

'We knew that Wes Brendel came from this town. He worked on a ranch with us five or six years ago. So me and Mike figured as how he'd be headin' right back home. And we was the only folks what had spotted him in Tombstone.'

'Sounds fine,' Luke said slowly, 'but why did you figure him for the robbery?'

'He's a troublemakin' no-good. Got thrown outa every job he ever had for stealin' from folks. We reckoned as how he'd raided the store and then come back here to hide the guns until he could get across the border to Mexico and sell them to some rich city folks who wouldn't be askin' questions. And he used to boast about doin' things like that. We reckoned that five hundred dollars was worth pickin' up, Marshal.'

'If you lived to spend it.'

The man gave a sickly grin.

'Wes ain't no hand with a gun unless a fella has his back turned. We figured as how two of us could take him easy.'

'So why was you breakin' into Pete Drugget's store?' Luke asked.

'There was talk in your town of a burnt-out rig when we got here, and we started thinkin' about it. Then, while we was lookin' around town, we came across the gun-store. So we had us an idea. Suppose Wes stole the guns and sold them to this local fella. Don't that figure!'

'It might if you didn't know Pete Drugget.' Luke laughed. 'He's the least dishonest fella you ever did see. So you was breakin' in to see if the guns was there?'

'That's it, Marshal. That's the truth, as sure as the Almighty is lookin' down at us.'

The marshal looked hard at the man's eager face. Then he went over to his desk. He sat in silence for a few minutes, thinking deeply and almost unaware of the laboured breathing of the worried prisoner.

'Five hundred dollars is one hell of a lot of money,' he eventually said in a low voice. 'Those guns sure had to be somethin' mighty special.'

'I ain't no expert, Marshal, but we're talkin' fancy shotguns, sportin' rifles from England, and all sorts of high-class stuff. Mike had all the details in his pocket. Take a look-see, Marshal.'

'I'll do that.'

Luke Cassidy dimmed the lamps in the office

and left the jailhouse to see if the mortician was still in his funeral parlour. The lights were on in the double-fronted building and he knocked at the door, to be welcomed by the long-faced mortician.

He explained that he had come for whatever articles were in the pockets of the dead store-breaker. He waited while the mortician went to the back room to collect the few things that Mike had carried.

There was a pinchbeck watch, a packet of chewing-tobacco, a few coins, and a folded sheet of paper, which Luke seized eagerly. It was the reward poster. He read it under the light of the nearest oil-lamp. The list of nearly one hundred shotguns and rifles read like a catalogue of all the world's best firearms. Luke had heard tell of gun-makers like Lefaucheux, Greeners, Purdy, and Holland, and it was easy to understand that a reward of $500 was not excessive.

He had just finished reading it when Doc Hibbert came from the inner room.

'Just the man I wanted to see,' the medico said cheerfully. 'I got some news for you on the burnt-out body from the rig.'

'Was old Fred shot?' the marshal asked as he folded the sheet of paper and put it in his waistcoat pocket.

'Well, unless he'd growed a new set of teeth and sprouted six inches taller, I don't figure your corpse as bein' old Fred. If I had to make a guess, and judgin' from a partly melted brass ring on the little finger of the left hand, I'd say it was Wes Brendel we'll be buryin' tomorrow.'

SEVEN

Luke Cassidy ate his breakfast slowly. His eyes strayed from the warm food to the pleasing figure of his young wife as she bent over the stove, pouring water into the coffee pot. Their rooms above the jailhouse smelled sweet in the early morning light. They had only been married a short time, and he now realized that she was the only person in town to whom he could talk and pour out his troubles.

She turned and caught his glance. There was a smile on her face as she poured fresh coffee. His serious expression made her hesitate before she spoke.

'Something's worrying you, Luke,' she said then in a low voice. 'What is it?'

'Oh, just the job,' he murmured.

'More than that.' She leaned over the table and placed a hand on his arm. 'Tell me.'

He put down the coffee cup and looked into the warm blue eyes.

'It's this business with the stolen guns,' he said

64

slowly. 'It has to be some local fella who understands such things. Somebody with money. And it could be anybody in town. I just can't trust any of them now. I've always relied on the mayor, but when I was tellin' him about the wagon, and what the fella in the jailhouse said, I suddenly realized that Mayor Kroner could be as guilty as anyone.'

Ella Cassidy jumped up from the table and went back to the stove.

'Heavens to Betsy!' she said as she grabbed a skillet. 'I forgot you had a prisoner. I'd better get him some breakfast.'

Ella put on more bacon and prodded the sputtering rashers as she turned to face her husband.

'What do you think it's all about?' she asked.

That was what the lawman needed. Somebody who would listen and who could be trusted. He leaned his elbows on the table.

'Well, as I figure it,' he said, 'some fella from this town saw those fancy guns in Tombstone and decided to steal 'em. Now, I've checked on all our leadin' citizens, and they've all been outa town in the last few weeks. Any one of them could have been to Tombstone. Anyways, somebody hired Wes Brendel to do the job of breakin' into the store, loadin' the guns on a wagon, and drivin' it back here. I don't reckon to them riskin' comin' straight into town, so they arranged a meetin' in the canyon – and somethin' went wrong.'

'But the guns weren't on the wagon when you brought it into town,' Ella said, turning the bacon amid a flurry of spluttering fat.

'No,' he agreed. 'I reckon as how the load of whiskey was used to hide them, and when Wes Brendel reached the canyon, another wagon met him there and the guns were transferred. Then they left the load of liquor to be brought into town the next day. There was no hurry about that and nobody was likely to go through Dead Man's Canyon late at night.'

She smiled wryly. 'Except for the preacher in a hurry to get home,' she murmured.

'Exactly. And that's why it has to be somebody in town behind the whole thing. Once all the local folks knew about the wagon in the canyon, old Fred decided to beat us to it and load himself up with free liquor. And the fella who had brought the guns to the canyon decided to go out there as well. He needed to stop us examinin' the rig.'

Ella put the bacon on a large white plate, added some beans, and a few slices of bread.

'Take this down to your prisoner with some coffee before he figures we aim to starve him to death.'

Luke gulped down the last of his drink and did as he was told.

The young prisoner was sitting on his bunk, his thin, unshaven face bearing an expression of abject misery. He was just staring at the whitened ceiling when the marshal opened up and handed him the plate and a large mug of steaming coffee. The young man took it gratefully and was rather surprised when Luke Cassidy stood by the door with the keys swinging in his hand.

'Know anythin' about some liquor bein' stolen around Tombstone?' the lawman asked.

Hal Levitt had a fork raised to his mouth and paused to look at the marshal.

'Ain't heard tell of that,' he said quietly. 'Only them guns and some fellas as were bein' chased for horse-stealing. Why d'you ask, Marshal?'

Luke shrugged. 'Oh, just a passin' thought. Did you hear tell of how Wes Brendel would have got them guns outa Tombstone?'

'Reckon he had a rig lined up for the job,' he said. 'What's it got to do with liquor bein' stole?'

'Oh, it's just that we have a load of whiskey and brandy in the next cell, and it turned up all myste-rious-like. I was wonderin' if it had anythin' to do with Wes Brendel and Tombstone.'

He watched the man carefully but could detect no reaction to the idea of the two things being linked. Luke Cassidy decided to back his intuition.

'You was after the reward for those guns,' he said tentatively. 'Maybe you still have a chance of gettin' a share of it.'

The young prisoner's dark eyes brightened as he gazed at the lawman in sudden hope.

'You ain't gonna send me to trial?' he asked hoarsely.

'I was figurin' that if you helped me, maybe I could help you. Interested?'

'Sure am, Marshal. What do I have to do?'

'Well, now, I gotta talk to the mayor and the judge first of all. Make 'em see as you was just after the reward and not tryin' to rob Pete Drugget. If I can convince them of that, you'll be able to get the hell outa here. Then I want you to ride back to Tombstone and keepin' pokin' your nose into that robbery and Wes Brendel's part in it. But I also need to know about that load of liquor. You can dig into that as well. Who bought it; how did they pay, and what sort of rig they moved it in. Agreed?'

'Anythin' you say, Marshal. And I get a share of the reward if the guns are recovered?'

'If you and me can get them back without interference from other folk, we may be able to split that five hundred dollars between us.'

The man grinned for the first time.

'That sounds a good offer to me, Marshal. I won't let you down.'

'I know that, because I'll kill you if you do.'

Luke used his best chilling manner to drive the point home, and it seemed to work. The young man gulped noisily and hurriedly assured the lawman that he would not do anything amiss.

The mayor and the judge were hard to convince, but Luke managed it without giving too much away. A trial that would not end in a hanging was of little interest to the folks of Huyton township. And keeping prisoners locked up cost money. The result was that the young man rode out of town a couple of days later.

About an hour after he'd departed the marshal himself quietly left Huyton. He wanted another look at the burnt wagon. It had occured to him that close on a hundred guns would be a pretty heavy weight for one horse to pull. He calculated that the rig would have been drawn by a pair of animals as far as the canyon. Then the guns were moved on to another wagon and the liquor left to be collected and brought innocently into town later. He also reckoned that he knew why the wagon was burned.

The ride was a hot one in the blazing sun and dry wind that blew sharp dust across the trail. Luke was glad when Malvern Creek was reached and he could scoop up some cool water for himself while his mare took her fill.

The smell of burning still hung around as he looked at the wreckage with greater care than he had used last time. The tell-tale signs that he was searching for were there. Among the charred timbers that sagged over the distorted iron rims, he could see traces of a false flooring to the wagon. That was why it had been burned by whoever killed Wes Brendel.

He grinned contentedly, wiped his blackened hands on tufts of grass, and started for home.

Night had already fallen when he reached town and the main street was bathed in the warm glow that came from oil-lamps in the various buildings. The saloon was getting busy and would be noisier in an hour or so as the local ranch hands came in for their drink and women at the end of a hard week of herding cattle in the heat and dust of the range.

Luke sighed as he took his mount round to the corral and then opened up the office to settle himself at his desk for a long night of vigilance. He would patrol the town once or twice as the evening wore on. His badge would remind the drunks that there was some law and order in Huyton township.

He took out a pack of playing-cards and shuffled them in a rather half-hearted fashion. He was just about to deal himself a hand of solitaire when the door opened and Bill Harley entered with a furious expression on his thin face.

'I got me one hell of a deal here, Marshal,' he complained, leaning forward across the desk. 'Mosher Davis is putting it around that I brought that liquor into Huyton to ruin his business, and that I hired Wes Brendel to do the dirty work. Then I'm supposed to have killed Wes and burned the wagon. It don't make sense and I aim to take no more of it.'

Luke smothered a sigh of despair and tried to calm the situation.

'Look, Bill,' he said soothingly, 'just sit down a minute and don't go chasin' after Mosher. He's one nasty customer and he can use that gun he carries under his coat.'

'I can use a gun myself, and if you don't sort out

this liquor business, I'll sure as hell be payin' a call on him. Now, what's it to be?'

'Bill, there's one hell of a lot more to this than I can tell you. I've sent someone to Tombstone to make enquiries and we might know more in a few days. Just be patient. Mosher Davis could end up lookin' a real melon-head.'

The angry man subsided a little.

'Are you sure about that?' he asked. 'I ain't havin' my reputation dragged in the mud by a saloon-keeper who runs crooked card-games. And Wes Brendel was a fella more like to be workin' for Mosher than for me. I got a respectable hotel to run, and the Wes Brendels of the world don't fit in that kinda set-up.'

Luke Cassidy got up wearily from his desk.

'I'll go have a word with him,' he promised, 'and you get yourself home before you do somethin' you'll regret. Just leave it with me, Bill.'

He crossed the office to open the door and was on the point of ushering the hotel-owner out when a figure loomed from the darkness and forced a way into the jailhouse.

It was Mosher Davis, and an angry and flushed Mosher, who was pulling some small, unshaven man behind him. He stopped when he saw Bill Harley and hesitated for a moment before address-ing himself to the marshal.

'I got proof now!' he shouted as he pushed his companion forward. 'Chris Beatty here will bear me out, Marshal. This hotel fella bought that liquor to ruin my business. He can't get out of it now. Just ask Chris.'

Luke Cassidy raised a steadying hand and stepped between the two quarrelling men.

'Just hold it, Mosher,' he ordered sharply. 'Since we're all here, we'll thrash this business out quietly like decent folk. Now, start by tellin' me who you're pullin' round the town like a mule on a rope.'

The little man stepped forward and took a dirty Stetson off his grey, balding head. He held it to his sunken chest and looked at the lawman with watery eyes.

'I'm Chris Beatty, Marshal,' he said quietly. 'I don't know what in hell this is all about. I only came into town for a drink and some supplies. I'm from over San Cristobal way.'

Luke Cassidy recognized him now and nodded his greeting.

'Yeah, you're the fella who rents out wagons . . .'

He stopped in mid-sentence and took the little man none too gently by the arm.

'And you rented a rig to Wes Brendel,' he said as everything suddenly seemed to fall into place.

'That's right. All fair and square it was. Just as I was tellin' Mr Davis here.'

The little man was eager to clear himself of any blame for what had happened around town. Mosher Davis pushed forward, his voice loud and harsh.

'Now you got it, marshal,' he said. 'This hotel

fella sent Wes Brendel to hire a rig and then go get some liquor to bring quietly into town. He's gonna turn that run-down hotel of his into a saloon and ruin my business. I don't aim to let him get away with it.'

'I did no such thing!' the hotel-owner shouted. 'I never employed Wes Brendel and this fella's tellin' a pack of lies.'

Luke Cassidy had to push the two belligerent men away from each other. He held out a restraining hand to keep them apart. 'Now, just you two listen to me,' he said firmly. 'It ain't nothin' to do with the law if Bill Harley here wants to open a saloon. That's between the two of you, and that load of liquor ain't been seen to be stolen. It's just waitin' for a legal owner to claim it. And once that's settled, I don't give a hoot and a holler. But this wagon-rentin' fella is a different nest of tarantulas. I got me a few questions to ask him.'

He pushed Chris Beatty away from the two quarrelling men and ushered them firmly to the door. He flung it open and took each roughly by the elbow.

'Now, you two listen good,' he said quietly. 'You settle your differences peaceful-like and keep this town all nice and quiet the way the mayor and council want it. If you cause me any trouble, I'll have you both in the cells and feedin' on slops. My wife's already had to cook for one prisoner this week. I don't aim she should do it for two more. Now, get the hell outa here.'

Rather to his surprise, the two men meekly left the office and he slammed the door behind them. Little Chris Beatty stood by the stove, listening avidly and with his old hat like an untidy rag in his hands. Luke motioned him to a chair and poured out some coffee.

'Now, Chris,' he said with an attempt at putting the man at ease, 'I want you to tell me all about rentin' this rig to Wes Brendel. Just take it nice and slow and don't leave nothin' out.'

The little man was uneasy now. The office was warm and little trickles of sweat were running down his craggy face.

'I ain't done nothin' wrong, Marshal,' he said meekly. 'I just rent out rigs to all the smallholders in the area. My pa started the business when the loggin' was goin' a blast back in the sixties. It ain't the same now but I scrapes a livin' from it.'

'Chris, some of your rigs have a layer of planks on top of the real flooring. There's room between for all sorts of goodies. Know what I mean?'

The man looked slyly round the room as if for inspiration.

'Ain't nothin' unlawful about it,' he said defensively. 'Folks with valuables like to travel safe out on the range. I don't ask what they carries.'

'I know. You just rent out the wagons. And the one Wes Brendel took – that had a double bottom, didn't it?'

The man nodded glumly.

The marshal leaned forward across the desk.

'Would that hidin'-place have stored a hundred guns?' he asked.

'Guns!' The man looked genuinely shocked. 'Hell, no. I gave him that rig 'cause he didn't seem to need a wagon with a big hidin'-place. I felt he were just haulin' whiskey like Mr Harley ordered.'

'But there was a double bottom to the rig?'

'Sure, but it would only hold a few things. Not much more than a carpetbag would hold.'

'What sorta things are we talkin' about, Chris?'

The man shrugged.

'Whatever a fella wants to take into Mexico or bring back across the border,' he muttered. 'I don't ask them and they don't tell me.'

'I can imagine. And why did you think Mr Harley sent Wes Brendel to you?'

'The letter. Wes brought a letter from Mr Harley along with the money for hirin' a rig and one horse. I got it here.'

He reached eagerly into his waistcoat pocket and brought out a much-folded and creased piece of paper. Luke took it and instantly saw the printed heading of the Harley House Hotel across the top of the soiled sheet. It was a simple note asking Chris Beatty to hire out a rig to Wes Brendel and was clearly signed by Bill Harley. His florid signature ran across the bottom.

'Well, I guess that settles it,' the marshal muttered. He placed the missive on the desk and stroked it thoughtfully. He was about to ask the man whether the horse had been recovered when a volley of shots filled the night air and rattled the glass in the jailhouse windows.

EIGHT

Mosher Davis and Bill Harley left the marshal's office reluctantly. They stood at the hitching rail, glaring at each other in the dim light of the lamps that shone from nearby windows. Mosher's hand was on the butt of the concealed gun and his tight expression heralded danger at the least provocation.

It was Bill Harley who tried to make the peace.

'Mosher,' he said with quiet intensity, 'I never sent Wes Brendel to buy any liquor. That fella in there has it all wrong. I'm runnin' a high-class hotel and you and me cater for a different trade. We don't have to fight. This is all nonsense.'

'Chris Beatty came into town tonight and started drinkin' at my place,' Mosher retorted grimly. 'Folks told him about the burnt-out rig and he wondered if it was the one he rented to you. I questioned him, and he showed me a letter. You wrote it, askin' him to let Wes Brendel have a rig and a horse. It was on your letter-heading, bold as brass. You ain't foolin' me any, Bill Harley. I'll have you run outa this town before you know what's hit you. You've made a bad enemy. I'll be mayor in a year or so, and if you're still here, life won't be worth livin' for you.'

Bill Harley snorted. 'You talk big, Mosher,' he said tautly. 'Now I ain't a fightin' man, but I've had enough of this and I aim to protect my interests. I've never played at politics, but you'll be mayor over my dead body. I can promise you that.'

He turned to stalk away, but Mosher Davis caught him by the shoulder, swung him round, and hit the man full in the face. The hotel-owner fell against the rail, stumbled across the boarding and rolled on to the rutted dirt of the main street. Mosher Davis walked away with contempt written on his dark face. The few people in the street came to the aid of the fallen man and helped him back to the hotel.

He shook them off as he reached the door and, with blood running down his face, stumbled into the building. A couple of guests sitting there with drinks in their hands, looked up in alarm at the sight of the injured man and his expression of wild rage. He staggered across to the reception desk and reached beneath it to pull out a Colt .44.

One of the guests half-rose in his chair as though to stop him, but Bill Harley's blazing eyes made him halt and quietly sit down again.

The hotel-owner rushed across the street to the brightly lit Golden Chance. There were a few drinkers standing in the doorway and one of them ran inside to warn Mosher. The others parted like the Red Sea as the angry man rushed between them without appearing to be aware that they even stood there.

He stopped in the suddenly quiet saloon and looked around. The gun was cocked in his hand, and his face, now a mess of blood, was set like some death-mask. He tried to find Mosher Davis among the drinkers, but Mosher was not there. The man who had run inside with a warning now stood talking to one of the bartenders.

The bartender was a big man, used to handling drunks. He came round the counter with a pick-axe-handle in his large hand.

'Now, then, Mr Harley,' he said in a soothing voice. 'We don't want any trouble, do we?'

The hotel-owner peered at him before looking round the saloon once more.

'I've come for Mosher,' he said tightly. 'Get the bastard down here or I'll go lookin' for him.'

He made a move towards the stairs that led to the owner's living quarters, but the bartender blocked his way.

'The boss don't want to be disturbed,' he said warningly. 'Just go home and sleep it off.'

The hotel-owner was beyond reason. He raised the gun and pointed it at the man in front of him.

'Get outa my way!' he shouted. 'Get the hell outa my way!'

The bartender hesitated for a moment, his florid face a picture of doubt as he raised the pickaxe-handle as though to defend himself.

The shot took everybody by surprise. Bill Harley had pulled the trigger and the bartender staggered backwards against the stair rail. The pickaxe-handle dropped noisily to the sawdusted floor as he clutched the rail for support and blood oozed from a hole high in his neck. His face had gone pale and there was a moment of hushed shock before someone else in the room went for a gun.

Bill Harley saw the movement and swung on the man. He pulled the trigger again and sent him crashing into a table as the shot took him in the arm that had reached for the weapon.

There was panic now. Men were trying to get out of the line of fire. Some headed for the door and one jumped across the bar to hide behind it. Another bartender had produced a shotgun. Before he could use it, Bill Harley sent another shot in his direction and the man hastily ducked as he dropped the weapon.

It was Mosher Davis who put an end to it all. He appeared at the top of the stairs with his own pistol drawn and cocked. There was an expression of almost smug satisfaction on his face as he took careful aim and shot Bill Harley through the head. The hotel-owner dropped in a heap on the floor, the gun spinning a few yards away from his dying hand.

There was a long silence as Mosher came down the stairs and put his own gun away in its concealed holster.

'You all saw what happened,' he said calmly. 'I had to kill him before he shot anybody else. Sam, go get the doc.'

The bartender who had dropped the shotgun came forward eagerly.

'Shall I get the marshal as well?' he asked.

Mosher grinned. 'No, I figure him as bein' on his way. He'll sure as hell have heard the ruckus. In the meantime, the rest of us can have a well-deserved drink on the house.'

There was a general chorus of agreement, and while one bartender ran from the saloon, the other remaining barman began to set up the drinks.

Marshal Cassidy had jumped up from his chair in the jailhouse and grabbed a shotgun from the rack on the wall. He made a fierce gesture to Chris Beatty as he headed for the door.

'You stay put right there, fella,' he ordered. 'I still have some questions to ask you and you'd better have the right answers. So think things over until I get back.'

He ran across the street towards the Golden Chance. He had no need to ask from where the shots had originated. The crowd round the door of the saloon was enough to tell him that. Out of the corner of his eye he could see the sturdy figure of the mayor approaching from his store. At his side was the stouter outline of the local banker, Dave Lundigan. The money-lender wheezed and grunted as he tried to keep up with Mayor Kroner.

The heat inside the Golden Chance hit the lawman like a solid wall. He blinked in the lights for a moment and then saw the dead man on the floor and the two wounded who were now sitting up. The bartender looked in a bad way with a steady flow of blood from his neck wound and a face that was deathly white. The other man was not badly hurt and was already taking on the role of a local hero.

Everybody started explaining at once and it was soon clear that Mosher could not be arrested for merely defending himself and the other people in the saloon. By the time the talking had stopped and the drinking had started, the doctor was there with the mortician in eager attendance. Mayor Kroner and the banker were offered refreshment, as was the marshal. Nobody refused and the atmosphere grew thicker as they discussed what had been happening.

It was the banker who added something new to the story. He was a fatter version of the mayor, but moved around in a haze of Cologne and cigars. His face was sallow and his grey hair was neatly brushed and plentiful.

'I couldn't say anything earlier,' he said in a measured voice, 'but Bill Harley really was going to move in on Mosher's operation. He had it all planned out and came to me for help.'

'Why the hell didn't you tell me?' the mayor snapped angrily.

82

'I couldn't, Ned. It was bank business. You wouldn't like your affairs spread round the town, would you?'

The mayor looked a little sheepish while Luke Cassidy butted in to stop them arguing the point.

'What exactly happened, Mr Lundigan?' he asked.

'Well, Bill Harley came to my office one day and said that he was buying some goods in Tombstone and didn't want to send ready cash because it would be a transaction of several hundred dollars. So he asked for a bank-draft. I was only too willing to help. After all, the man had a sound business and was a good customer.'

'And then what?' It was the mayor who jumped in eagerly.

'He told me that he was planning on buying the empty store next to his place and knocking the two together. Then he was going to open a high-class saloon and serve quality liquor along with entertainment. It sounded like a fine business move and I reckoned as how it could do the town some good.'

'And do you some good, I shouldn't wonder,' the mayor grumbled. 'You should have told me, Dave. I had a right to know. I'd have told you both that Mosher wasn't the sort of fella to take that lightly. A shootin' like we've just had was waitin' to happen.'

'So Bill Harley went to Tombstone and bought the liquor?' Luke asked patiently.

'Yes,' the banker agreed, 'and Wes Brendel was presumably hired to bring it back here.'

The mayor looked from one man to the other.

'And they left it in the canyon until after dark,' he mused, 'so that they could bring it in without Mosher gettin' wind of it.'

He made it sound as if a great truth had dawned.

'Exactly,' the banker said unhappily. 'But something seems to have gone wrong.'

'So who killed Wes Brendel?' the mayor asked.

They both looked at the marshal but he only shrugged. He was as confused as they were.

'I got Chris Beatty in the office,' he said, 'and there's still a few questions I need to ask him.'

He left them after finishing his drink and retired to the jailhouse where Chris still sat hunched in his chair looking pretty fed up with everything. The marshal put the shotgun back in the rack and sat down at his desk.

'Now, Chris,' he said, 'why did you give Wes a wagon that had a secret compartment?'

The man shrugged. 'All my wagons are built like that,' he said. 'That's how I make my living.'

'Did Wes know that?'

'Sure. We done business a few times.'

'Did he ask for a particular wagon, or did he leave it to you?'

The question took the man by surprise and he had to think about it for a moment.

'Well, like I told you, Marshal, he didn't seem to

84

care none. Just took the first I offers. Maybe he weren't carryin' nothin' you might call dishonest, eh?'

'And maybe he sang in the preacher's choir. Has your horse found its way home yet?'

'No, it ain't, and my wagon's all burned out. Who's gonna pay for all that? I sure as hell can't afford them sorta losses.'

'You're in a risky business, Chris.' The marshal grinned. 'Some of the folk you deal with are right dishonest.'

'I'll sure as hell tell the world they are. Can I go now?'

'Sure. And take my advice. Just hire your rigs out to the timber fellas in future.'

'There ain't no money in haulin' timber.'

'Maybe not, but you could live longer.'

A sudden thought struck the marshal as the man got up to leave.

'Just one more thing, Chris,' he said hurriedly. 'Was old Fred Brown with Wes when he picked up the wagon?'

Chris Beatty shook his head.

'No, ain't seen old Fred in a coon's age.'

NINE

Bill Harley's funeral was a big affair. All the worthies of the town turned out for it and sang the hymns lustily in the little burial plot behind the clapboard meeting-house. Obadiah Scrubbs officiated with all the gruesome enjoyment he derived from threatening hell and damnation to everyone who did not support his views. His halo of grey hair waved in the light wind as he clutched the Bible to his bony chest and orated at great length despite a gesture from the mayor to get a move on.

Mosher Davis had the good manners not to attend, but he was one of the few absent from the event. Mrs Harley stood at the graveside in deepest black and wiped her eyes with a large lace handkerchief. Her two daughters accompanied her, their plain faces awash with tears.

Marshal Cassidy walked slowly back to the jailhouse when it was all over. Ella stayed behind to talk to some of her friends and get all the latest gossip.

His office was cool at that time of the day with

the sun shedding its light and heat on the other side of the street. Luke sat down at his desk with a cup of coffee and was almost dozing off when the door opened and Mrs Harley stood on the threshold. She was alone, and the marshal rose hurriedly to offer her a chair. This was what he had been dreading; an angry widow demanding that the killer of her husband be brought to justice.

'Now that everything's in the open,' she said in a calm and businesslike voice, 'I sent into Tombstone for a copy of the receipt Wes Brendel collected for my husband. I guess the original burned with Wes. It's for the liquor my Bill purchased. It now belongs to me, I believe.'

Luke opened his mouth to say something but words failed to come. He just nodded dumbly and took the piece of paper from her hand. It was from an auction house and was for $264 with an added note that the goods were to be collected later by Wes Brendel for delivery to Huyton township. He handed the receipt back slowly.

'It all belongs to you, ma'am,' he said. 'Was you figurin' on sellin' it off? I'm told it's worth more than your husband paid, and you might do well out of a sale in town.'

She snorted angrily, her plain face puckered in a grimace of contempt.

'Only Mosher Davis would be buyin' in this one-horse place,' she said, 'and I ain't figurin' on lettin' him have the last laugh. No, Marshal, I aim to finish what Dave Lundigan tells me my Bill started. I'm goin' into the saloon business because I got a score to settle with Mosher. If I can't get the son-of-a-bitch one way, I'll get him another.'

'He's a dangerous man, Mrs Harley,' Luke ventured.

'And I'm a dangerous woman,' she snapped. 'This town will grow, and me and Bill always aimed to be part of it. It were my pa's money what set us up in the hotel and Bill worked hard to make it what it is today. I reckoned as how he might be mayor in a few years, and we'd be looked up to as folks with a pioneerin' spirit. Well, me and my girls aim to do what Bill started, and all the Moshers in the world won't stop us.'

Luke gazed at the determined woman with frank admiration.

'I like that, ma'am,' he said with a grin, 'and I'm sure on your side. Would you like me to arrange delivery of the liquor to the Harley House?'

'Ain't no hurry, Marshal. I just looked in now before that preacher fella gets ideas about bein' the finder.'

Luke grinned again and rose from the chair to accompany her to the door.

'I reckon he was hopin' to make a dollar or two,' he said. 'Just leave it with me, ma'am. It's safe here.'

He watched her walk stiffly along the street with men raising their hats in respect as she passed.

'That sure is some woman,' Luke murmured to

himself. He refilled his coffee cup and warmed his hands on it.

The mayor and the councilmen seemed to think that it was all over. Luke Cassidy was not so sure. He still wondered why Wes Brendel had been killed and what had happened to old Fred Brown. He also wondered why the wagon had been burned. Nothing was solved, so far as he could see, and he fretted over the problem for the next few days.

He had to accept that Bill Harley had bought the liquor and was going to open up another saloon, but would Bill Harley kill Wes Brendel? And why would he burn the rig if he was not smuggling something in the hidden compartment? It did not make sense and the marshal gnawed away at the problem without success.

And there was the most important thing of all. Where were the guns?

The answer to that came on the following Monday. He opened up his office at nine in the morning, watched the children on their way to the misery of the schoolhouse, and then settled down at the desk to write his monthly report. It was a job he hated, forming the words in a large, slow hand and spilling blots on the paper as he laboured at it.

He heard the horse drawing up outside and saw the shadow of a man fall across the window as he tethered the animal to the hitching rail. Luke waited in pleasurable anticipation at the prospect of a visitor who would take him away from the writing chore.

The visitor was young Hal Levitt, covered in dust and not looking particularly cheerful as he took the cup of coffee gratefully and sat down opposite the marshal.

'You look like the turkey-shoot paid out in Confederate dollars,' Luke said in an attempt to cheer him up a little.

'Well, I sure as hell ain't bein' paid out the five-hundred-dollar reward, Marshal,' the young man grated as he sipped the hot liquid. 'They got the guns back. They was never properly stole.'

Luke leaned forward. 'You'd better tell me the whole story,' he suggested.

The young man sighed. 'Where shall I start?' he asked.

'As it was in the beginning,' the marshal suggested in an effort to lighten the situation. His gesture was wasted and Hal still looked miserable as he began his story.

'Well, the store was broke into and the guns took the night Wes Brendel was in Tombstone. Marshal Earp got things organized as soon as he heard, and every rig leavin' town was searched. They really did all they could, even sendin' fellas out in every direction to try and pick up a trail.'

He paused to take a drink.

'They didn't search the rig Wes was drivin' because he'd left town much earlier. Before anybody raised the alarm. Anyhows, a fella ridin' into Tombstone a few days later comes across the guns just lyin' in a heap of cactus. They was all covered in sand and some was beginnin' to rust. The fella what owns them is real sore. He figures as how they're not worth a half of their value no more. So we gets no reward, Marshal.'

'I guess not.'

Luke studied the man in silence for a few moments.

'Why did you come back here, Hal?' he asked quietly.

'I said I would, didn't I? You gave me a chance last week, and I don't aim to let you down. I ain't a thief and I'd like to be in steady work.'

Luke nodded. 'And I'd be happy to take you on as deputy, but the councilmen don't like spendin' money except on themselves. And you ain't exactly a dead shot with a gun.'

The man grinned wearily.

'Ain't that the truth,' he agreed.

'I do have another little job for you though. It'll just pay posse money. Interested?'

Hal brightened up. 'Sure am.'

'There's an old fella gone missin' from town. Fred Brown is his name and he has a scraggy mule and a dog with him. If he's still alive, I want him found. He can't have travelled far. He ain't got much money but he's got a tall thirst. Now, I figure that Wes Brendel scared him outa town. I reckon as how he could be in one of those old cabins up on the tree-line, or maybe down in the old gold-diggings. Somewhere near drinkin' water and not too far from a saloon. See what you can do, Hal, and tell him it's safe to come home.'

The young man got up to go shortly afterwards. He had arranged to spend the night in a shed behind the jailhouse. As he headed for the door, he stopped in mid-stride.

'I don't know whether this is important, Marshal,' he said uncertainly, 'but don't the stage come into town tomorrow?'

'Yes, some time in the afternoon. Why?'

'There was a fella in Tombstone, real tough-lookin' character he was, and he was in and out the marshal's office. Seemed all palsy with the law back there. He went into the Wells Fargo office just as I was leavin' town, and I have me the feelin' that he was some sort of official-type fella. Sheriff or federal marshal, perhaps. Dressed like some big-town dude, all cut-away coat, fancy waistcoat, and gold watch-chain. But two guns, Marshal, and he sure as hell looked like he knew how to use 'em.'

'Got a name for him?'

'The Wells Fargo clerk was callin' him Mr Martin, and bein' mighty polite about it.'

TEN

The stage came in an hour late on Thursday afternoon. It drew up in front of the Wells Fargo office in a haze of dust and a flurry of excitement from the folk who wanted the latest news from other towns. Luke Cassidy watched from his office. He saw the mail-bag and the bundles of newspapers handed over and noted the luggage being passed down to waiting hands. There were only three passengers: an elderly couple who were returning from a family wedding, and a tall, slimly built man who paused on the boardwalk to look around. His narrowed eyes missed nothing as he waited for the large carpetbag to be placed at his feet.

He was much as Hal Levitt had described him. His coat, even though covered in dust, was well fitted and partly hid a chamois waistcoat that housed a large watch-chain. His face was dark and saturnine, with deep creases at either side of a thin mouth. He had a slightly greying moustache and it could have been easy to guess that his age would be around the fifty mark. He wore dark leather gloves despite the heat and there were two guns at his waist.

Luke Cassidy knew who Cass Martin was. He had heard the name often enough but had never met the man. He knew of him as a ruthless bounty hunter who skirted close to defying the law and had killed several men in order to make a profit. He was a friend of the Earp family, and particularly of the reckless third brother, Morgan.

The new arrival picked up the carpetbag and said something to the Wells Fargo clerk. The man pointed up the main street and received a nod of thanks. Cass Martin set off in the direction indicated to arrive in front of the Harley House Hotel a few moments later. He looked the building up and down and then went inside.

The hotel was a calm place that smelled clean and housed brightly polished furniture and gilded mirrors to reflect the light of the large copper oil-lamps that hung from shiny brass chains. There were potted plants and a mahogany reception desk where Ma Harley stood with a thin smile on her plain and calculating face.

'Welcome to the Harley House,' she said as she eyed the man in front of her. 'I got a nice room right away from the noise of the street. How long you staying?'

Cass Martin's glance was as cold and calculating as her own.

'Is Bill Harley around?' he asked.

A guarded look came over her face as she studied the man.

'No, he ain't around,' she said slowly. 'I'm his wife.'

'He bought some liquor in Tombstone,' the visitor said in his dry, cold voice, 'and I aim to talk to him about it.'

'Do you now? Well, he ain't talkin' to nobody. We buried him the other day.'

Cass Martin's mouth opened to curse but he managed to control himself in time.

'Too bad,' he said slowly. 'My condolences, ma'am.'

Ma Harley leaned on the desk.

'So, what do you want, fella?' she asked. 'You ain't here to take no rest-cure, so spit it out.'

'You speak mighty plain, ma'am,' Cass Martin said with just the vestige of a smile. 'Maybe I'd like to look at this liquor.'

'Have you seen the marshal?' Ma Harley asked bluntly.

'No, I got no truck with marshals.'

'Is that a fact, now. So what would you be after?'

'A deal.'

He was closer to her now and she could smell the tobacco on his breath.

'And what sort of deal would that be?' she asked quietly. 'You settin' up in the saloon business?'

'I ain't interested in the liquor, ma'am. It's the other things I want. And I aim to get them.'

She studied the man coldly.

'Do you now?' she mused. 'I figure as how the marshal might be interested in you, fella. I think I'll go call on him.'

She lifted the flap at the end of the reception desk and was just about to step out when she found herself facing the barrel of a Colt .44 held in a steady, gloved hand.

'I aim to look at that load of liquor, ma'am, and I aim to search until I find what I'm lookin' for. It don't pay to stand in my way. Nothin' personal. Just business.'

Ma Harley looked at the gun that was levelled within a few inches of her ample breast. She gave the man a tight smile as she peered over his shoulder.

'Well,' she said, 'I'm a defenceless widow woman with two daughters, since my husband died last week. But my daughters ain't so defenceless, and Maisie is standin' right behind you with a shotgun like to blow your ass off. So the best thing you can do, fella, is to put that thing away before she lets fly.'

Cass Martin hesitated for a moment and then glanced at one of the mirrors that reflected the girl who stood silently on the thick carpet with a short-barrelled shotgun aimed at his back. He put the pistol slowly into its holster and shrugged expressively.

'You play a careful game, ma'am,' he conceded, 'so now we talk on equal terms.'

'That sounds better,' Ma Harley said with a

slight smile. 'Let's go sit over there and take a drink. We don't want any of the guests to think we're fightin' and feudin' in a nice place like this, do we?'

She led the way to a small table by the window while her daughter took the mother's place behind the reception desk. The shotgun was hidden from sight and the other daughter quickly brought over a couple of whiskey-glasses. Some water was added to Ma Harley's drink for the sake of appearances and the two sat opposite each other, calculating their positions.

'Now, suppose you tell me what all this is about?' the hotel-owner suggested.

'A load of liquor was bought in Tombstone by your husband, ma'am, and it was brought here by a fella called Wes Brendel. Now, I want to see that liquor. I hear tell that Brendel was killed and the wagon burned out. So that just leaves you. Where's the liquor, ma'am?'

There was a slight silence as Ma Harley worked out the details in her mind.

'I would have thought the marshal—' she began.

'No, I don't share with no lawman.'

'Share? You one of them bounty hunters?' Ma Harley was interested now.

'Some folks call me that.'

'Buyin' liquor don't call for no rewards, unless . . .' she stopped in mid-sentence.

'Unless, ma'am?'

'Unless there was somethin' else on the wagon.'

He nodded agreement.

'You got it, ma'am,' he said quietly, 'and I ain't above sharin' the reward with someone as helps me find it.'

Ma Harley took a deep swig of her drink and sat back comfortably in her chair. She could see things clearly now and her calculating mind was working overtime.

'You're right about keepin' clear of the marshal,' she said. 'He's one greedy fella where rewards are concerned. Now, I ain't got that liquor 'cos my husband never did buy it. We're hotel folk, not saloonkeepers.' She leaned forward confidentially. 'The fella you're lookin' for is called Mosher Davis. He runs the Golden Chance and he used my husband's name to make things look respectable. One hell of a dust-up there was when Bill found out. That's how he got himself shot. Mosher killed him.'

The look on Cass Martin's face told her all she wanted to know. She had hooked him.

'I've heard tell of Mosher Davis,' he said thoughtfully, 'and Wes Brendel was his sorta folk.'

Ma Harley nodded. 'Worked for Mosher on and off for years,' she said. 'They musta used the liquor to hide whatever it is you're lookin' for. They forged my man's name to hire a rig and buy the load. Then Mosher killed Wes and burned the rig. Bill went across to the saloon to face him down, and Mosher pulled a gun. They called it a fair fight

98

and that damned lawman didn't do nothing. So, look out for Mosher. He'll kill you as soon as spit. I'd get some back-up before tacklin' him if I was in your boots, fella.'

The man's head pulled back in a gesture of contempt. Ma Harley had hit the right note by challenging his ability to tackle the saloonkeeper. She knew at that moment that he would not go to the law for any help.

'I'll leave my bag here,' Cass Martin said, rising from his seat, 'and I'll go pay a visit to this saloon fella.'

Ma Harley rose as well.

'He has two bartenders now,' she said. 'There's a shotgun and a couple of axe-handles beneath the counter. Mosher has a gun under his coat, and he's right-handed.'

Cass Martin nodded. 'Thank you, ma'am,' he said formally.

Ma Harley watched the man leave and was joined by her daughter to stand at the window and follow his movements as he crossed the street to where the Golden Chance stood in all its garish paintwork.

'You played that well, Ma,' Maisie said with a wide grin.

'I surely did,' her mother agreed. 'Mosher owes me, and I aim to make him pay for your pa's death. That fella looks just the man to do it.'

The other daughter looked doubtful.

'What if Mosher kills him?' she asked.

'That's nothin' to us.'

'Or what if he finds out that Mosher never bought that liquor? He's apt to come back here lookin' for trouble.'

Ma Harley patted her daughter's arm reassuringly.

'A fella who molests helpless women is fair game. We ain't none of us fresh outa the cracker-barrel, and I reckon he'd be dead before he got through that door.'

They all laughed at the prospect and saw the swing-doors of the Golden Chance close behind Cass Martin as he entered the saloon.

The place was nearly empty at that time of day and only one bartender was on duty. Two men stood at the bar while three more sat at a table talking in low voices. They looked up at the entry of the stranger.

Cass Martin's right hand was resting on the butt of his gun as he surveyed the room with cold distaste. He looked at the uneasy bartender and the temperature of the saloon seemed to have dropped under the quiet menace of his dead eyes.

'Mosher Davis,' he said in a flat voice.

'He ain't here,' the bartender answered nervously. He glanced around as though looking for help.

Cass Martin glanced at the stairs and door at the top that led to the living-quarters. He started in that direction and the worried bartender found his voice.

'You can't go up there,' he ventured.

Cass Martin turned. 'If you make a move for that shotgun you got under the counter, I'll blow your head off,' he answered quietly.

The man's hands stayed on the bar top as he watched in fascination while the customers decided it was time to leave discreetly.

Mosher was sitting in a large brocaded armchair with the newly arrived Tombstone newspapers spread in front of him. He looked up in surprise at the sudden intrusion of the stranger.

'What the hell do you want, fella?' he shouted, rising from the chair.

Cass Martin's gun cut him short. It was pointed at the saloon keeper's stomach and held in a steady hand.

'I got questions to ask.'

Mosher sat down again, letting the papers drop to the floor. His own gun was down on the left side of the chair, lying in its holster just in reach of his hand if he could lean over. He knew that he had to play for time and divert attention to reach it.

'What questions?' he asked in a reasonable voice. 'I never met you that I know of.'

'It's about that load of liquor that came from Tombstone,' Cass Martin told him. 'I want what came with it.'

Mosher frowned in puzzlement.

'I can't help you there,' he said in bewilderment. 'I only saw it once, and it was just bottles and crates. Nothin' else. What exactly are you after, fella?'

'You know well enough, and I don't aim to play games.'

Mosher Davis was no coward. He rose to his feet, letting the barrel of the gun brush against his waistcoat as he glared hard at Cass Martin.

'Now, you just listen good and hard, fella,' he said in a menacing tone. 'You're in my town, on my territory. And if you're fool enough to start any shootin' here, there's plenty of folk will finish it for you. Now, put that away and tell me what this is all about.'

Cass Martin stared at the man before him. Mosher was a hard, tough-looking character whose cold eyes were as deadly as his own. There was a moment of deadlock before the intruder lowered the pistol slightly.

'You got delivery of somethin' else as well as the liquor,' he said tersely. 'We both know how things are, and I aim to make me a profit outa this deal. One way or another. Now, you can hand it all over or I get real rough.'

Mosher was a shrewd enough judge to see how the man was backing down. His own curiosity and greed were aroused, and he decided to put out a few feelers.

'Well, you got yourself a problem there,' he said softly. 'You can't do any shootin' without bringin' the whole town in on us, so I reckon that we have some tradin' to do.'

102

Mosher sat down again, leaning back in his chair with his left arm draped over the side so that his hand was within six or eight inches of the gun.

'I'll cut you in for ten per cent of the reward,' Cass Martin said with just a hint of desperation in his voice.

Mosher smiled. He knew that he was master of the situation now.

'Ten per cent don't sound much to me,' he mused. 'Let's make it fifty.'

There was a long silence as the saloon-owner slumped comfortably and watched his opponent sweating in the warmth of the well-appointed room. The smell of cooking was strong and the ticking of a wall clock seemed loud in the confined space.

It was Cass Martin who made the next move.

'I can always do a deal with the marshal,' he said slowly. 'And you'd go to jail. Just havin' that stuff is enough to put you behind bars for the rest of your life.'

Before Mosher could think of an answer, the door from the kitchen opened noisily.

Cass Martin turned in alarm and Mosher reached down for the short-barrelled Colt. He swung out of the chair with it grasped in his left hand. The noisy cocking of the hammer made the visitor look back again, caught between two possible enemies. Mosher pulled the trigger as he saw his opponent's gun swing in his direction. There was a shriek from the open doorway of the kitchen and two more shots were exchanged.

The noise was deafening in the low-ceilinged room. A haze of acrid powder filled the air and a soft moaning came from the woman who had collapsed on the carpet. The pan of boiling water had fallen from her hand as she tried to throw it at Cass Martin. Most of it had gone wide and his shot had taken her just above the waistline of her white apron.

Mosher had fallen back in the chair, the gun still in his hand but his eyes glazing as he breathed his last. Cass Martin was the only survivor. He had outshot them both and now headed for the door before the law could be alerted to the noise. He threw it open and hurried down the stairs into the bar. The place was empty and he looked around to see if there was a back way out. There was no sign of a rear exit and he hesitantly moved towards the swing-doors that fronted the main street.

Marshal Cassidy was waiting for him.

ELEVEN

The marshal's shotgun was pointing steadily at the man who stood in the doorway of the Golden Chance. And there were other guns on the street. The whole town seemed to have gathered behind Luke Cassidy. Most of them stood at a safe distance but a few of the men had drawn their pistols and one wagon driver was pointing his own shotgun with both hammers cocked and an almost wistful look of anticipation on his bearded face.

Cass Martin cursed himself for his ill-luck. He spread his arms wide to show that he did not intend to fight.

'There's been a shooting,' he explained in as calm a voice as he could muster. 'That Mosher fella drew on me and I had to fire back, Marshal. I ain't lookin' for trouble, so I'll go along to your jail-house all quiet-like. It was just a private quarrel.'

'Drop your gun belt,' Luke ordered.

The man did as he was told and stepped foward while one of the onlookers collected it and went to stand by the marshal.

The mayor was there, with Dave Lundigan on one side and Doc Hibbert on the other. The medical man lumbered up the wooden steps and entered the saloon, pushing the swing-door with one hand and grasping his bag in the other. Luke Cassidy waved his gun at the prisoner and let him lead the way down the street towards the jailhouse. Cass Martin was locked up while the crowd hovered uncertainly between that building and the Golden Chance saloon.

The marshal put the shotgun back in its rack and stepped out on the street again. The townsfolk were now gathering outside the saloon while the mortician's cart was already there with a wooden casket on board in the hope that it might be needed.

As the lawman reached the building, the mortician's assistant came out to pick up the casket from the cart. Somebody asked him if Mosher was really dead and the young man nodded as he shouldered the heavy wooden box.

'His wife's been shot too,' he said in an attempt not to sound too cheerful. 'Hurt real bad.'

The change of mood in the crowd was almost tangible. Curiosity had been the dominating thing until that moment. Mosher was not a popular man and many of the churchgoers disapproved of a saloon anyway. But now it was different. A woman had been injured, and there was an audible murmur on the street.

Marshal Cassidy entered the building and went

up the stairs. He looked round the room where Mosher lay. Doc Hibbert was giving emergency treatment to Mrs Davis while the mortician stood over Mosher's body. The mayor was also there with the bank president, both staring aimlessly around at the comfort of the place with its Eastern-bought furniture and fine carpets. The curtains were heavy velvet and there were books and ornaments on an elaborate series of shelves. Mosher had lived well.

The lawman took in the situation as he noticed the pan, the spilled water, and Mosher's fallen gun. The acrid smell of burnt powder was still in the air and he turned to see how the doctor was coping.

The medical man shook his head sadly as he asked the mortician's assistant to help him carry Ma Davis to the bedroom where he could do a better job of trying to save her life.

Mayor Kroner came over to Luke and took him gently by the arm to whisper confidentially into his ear.

'Folks are goin' to get pretty riled about this,' he pointed out. 'Shootin' Mosher is one thing. But a woman! There could be a lynching, and we gotta stop it.'

'I reckon you're right, Mayor,' Luke agreed. 'But I got me no deputies.'

The bank president put in an anxious comment.

'You could deputize a few men,' he suggested. 'The council would pay. Just for a day or two.'

Luke pursed his lips.

'The sorta fellas I'd need would be the very ones leadin' a lynchin' party,' he pointed out unkindly. He stared hard at the two prominent citizens. 'Of course, if some of the councilmen volunteered, it would sure impress folk,' he went on. 'I got a few badges if you'd like to come along and join me.'

The bank president went a little pale and the mayor blinked rapidly. He looked round the room as if searching for inspiration.

'Now, as I see it,' he said judicially, 'this could have been a fair shoot-out between the two men. Ma Davis comes outa the kitchen with a pan of water, gets caught in the crossfire, and could have been shot by either of them. Maybe we're gettin' too excited about the whole thing.'

'You mean that I should let the fella leave town?'

The two men nodded eagerly.

Before they could discuss the matter further, the doctor came into the room. He was wiping his hands on a towel and shook his head as he approached them.

'You'll need another casket,' he told the mortician.

'Did she say anything?' the mayor asked with unfeeling eagerness. 'Tell you how she was caught in the crossfire?'

'Didn't even pass the time of day,' Doc Hibbert said drily.

Banker Lundigan looked from the mayor to the medical man.

'Does anybody know what the shootin' was all about!' he asked.

All eyes were fixed on Luke Cassidy but he decided to play it discreetly.

'The fella came in on the stage,' he said quietly, 'so I reckon it must have been an old quarrel that brought him here.'

The banker nodded thankfully. 'Then I reckon the mayor's right,' he said in a relieved voice. 'It's all over and don't concern the town. Let this fella get on his horse and go his way. A lynching would be bad for the town's reputation, and a trial costs money.'

'He ain't got a horse,' the marshal said patiently. 'He came in on the stage.'

'Well, use any horse you have in the corral,' the mayor snapped edgily. 'Let's just get him the hell outa here.'

The three men left the room and walked slowly down the stairs. The crowd had shifted now and was gathered round the jailhouse. The door of the building was open and Luke instantly guessed that the ringleaders were already inside. He had left the keys in his desk and the whole town knew they were kept there. He stood alongside the mayor and the banker, undecided between duty and the sure knowledge that he could not prevent what was going to happen.

It was Mayor Kroner who made the decision.

'We can't stop 'em,' he said sensibly, 'and them folks all have a vote next year. I suggest we take ourselves a drink at the bar.'

The banker nodded and was the first to turn in that direction. Luke Cassidy took one last glance before joining them at the counter where the mayor picked out the best bottle of whiskey and poured out generous helpings.

The mortician and his helper brought the casket downstairs and deposited it on the sawdusted floor while they came across to join the others at the bar. The mayor poured out some whiskey for them and the little group drank in silence.

The mortician's assistant crossed to the window and looked out at what was happening on the main street. The excitement on his face communicated itself to his boss who went to join him.

'Have we got a spare casket made up?' the mortician asked doubtfully.

'Ma Edgeton won't be needin' hers for a few days or so,' the young man replied. 'If he ain't too tall, we could use that.'

'He don't look so tall,' his boss mused, 'and it ain't gonna be a fancy send-off.' He looked at the mayor. 'Not if the town's payin' the bill.'

The others joined the two men at the window and looked out at the crowd which was now coming back along the street to the grain-store where the loading-boom stuck out and where a rope could be slung with very little effort. There was a prisoner being held in firm hands as he struggled amid the shouting crowd. The women screeched abuse and children danced wildly on the fringe of the mob as if it was some special treat.

Luke Cassidy turned away. He felt ashamed at not being able to do anything. He not only felt shame, he felt a great degree of annoyance. There were questions he had wanted to ask Cass Martin. He wanted to know why his first call had been on the widow Harley. And what a bounty hunter was doing in Huyton township.

He heard a sudden burst of applause from the street and was unable to resist going back to the window. The man had been hanged, and was swinging high in the air, kicking and twitching while the townsfolk celebrated. Then he gave a little shiver that seemed to run the length of the rope. His body hung still and lifeless as the crowd stared.

There was a sudden silence in which not even the children uttered a sound. It seemed to last a long time, and then a single voice began to sing a hymn. It was the preacher.

It was late afternoon when Luke Cassidy ventured into the refined atmosphere of the Harley House hotel. Ma Harley greeted him with one of her automatic smiles as he leaned across the reception desk.

'Why did Cass Martin come to see you, Ma?' he asked.

'He wanted a room is why,' she replied calmly. 'I'm runnin' a hotel, Marshal.'

'Is his bag still here?'

'Sure is. You claimin' it?'

He nodded and waited while she lifted the large carpetbag from under the desk.

'Any idea why he went to see Mosher?' he asked.

The woman smiled. 'I wouldn't know, Marshal. Maybe they was old friends.'

'Maybe. You and Mosher had quite a score to settle. Seems to be settled now.'

'I reckon so. Justice works out in funny ways, don't it.'

Luke Cassidy took the bag and left the hotel.

There were three funerals the next day. Two of them were as elaborate as the town could have wished for. Mosher's estate was paying the bill and the mortician skimped nothing. The other was done later, as dusk was setting over the hills. Only the marshal attended when Cass Martin was lowered into the earth. The lawman walked slowly back to his office with the noise of the spades, echoing around the nearly empty street as the dirt was shovelled on top of the plain casket.

Luke could smell his wife's cooking wafting down from the upper floor. He went to sit at his desk, knowing that she would stamp on the boards when the meal was ready. He had his work-book to fill in and he pulled it out of the drawer reluctantly.

The discreet tap on the back door was so gentle that he was uncertain about it until the sound was

112

repeated. The lawman got up from his chair and went down the corridor to investigate. A solitary figure stood there in the darkness, and it took a moment for him to realize that it was a dust-covered Hal Levitt.

The young man grinned as he entered the office.

'I found Fred Brown, Marshal,' he said cheer-fully.

TWELVE

It was a ride of nearly four hours to Penitent Creek. The sun was high and the sharp wind blew almost horizontally across the parched earth. Luke Cassidy was cursing inwardly at having to make a journey that might be a waste of time.

Hal Levitt had not brought Fred Brown back to Huyton township. The old man was safely tucked away by the creek in one of the cabins used by the panhandlers twenty years ago and now deserted and falling down. He was scared to go back to town, and Hal Levitt had not even been able to get near him. The old drunk had fired at him with a shotgun and warned him to keep his distance. The young man had shouted his message, telling him that the marshal of Huyton township had sent him and that it was safe to return home again. Wes Brendel was dead.

Old Fred hesitated to believe it, and sent word back to the lawman. He was to come himself to Penitent Creek, fire a single shot when he got there, and wait until Fred had checked him out as the genuine article. Hal Levitt grinned as he delivered the news, but Luke just cursed at the stubborness of the old sinner.

Like it or not, he did what Fred required and arrived at the creek in the early afternoon. There were five cabins still standing. Two of them had some roofing but the others looked totally derelict. There was no sign of life save for a few birds of prey flying high against the sun and a scurry of lizards in front of the approaching horse.

Luke Cassidy peered around carefully before unholstering his Colt and pulling back the hammer. He fired a single shot in the air and put the gun away again. The birds wheeled off into the distance, a jackrabbit scuttled between two of the cabins, but nothing else happened. The marshal waited patiently while his horse pawed the ground and scattered white streams of sweat from its mouth.

'Fred!' Luke Cassidy shouted loudly. 'I ain't got all day so show yourself, you old coyote.'

He heard a noise behind him and swung in the saddle to see the old man emerge from a clump of bushes. He held a shotgun steadily as he screwed up his eyes to look at the visitor. Then his bearded face broke into a grin.

'Well, I reckon as how it really is you, Marshal,' he said, lowering the weapon. 'Gotta be careful at my age. Ain't as fast on the trigger as I used to be. Come and have a cup of coffee.'

He led the way to one of the roofed cabins and

waited in the doorway while Luke dismounted, loosened the girth of his horse, and tethered it to a piece of jutting timber. The marshal followed the old man into the hut and was surprised to find it clean and with a decent bed against one wall. There was a table and some stools, with a small stove in one corner. A coffee pot bubbled away on top of it and Fred poured a couple of mugs while the lawman took one of the stools and rested his elbows on the rough table top.

'You've made yourself comfortable here, Fred,' he said as he sipped. 'You got my message. Wes Brendel is dead and it's safe to come back to Huyton.'

The old man's eyes were shrewd as he looked over the top of his own mug.

'What makes you think I'm hidin' from him?' he asked.

'Well, now, I ain't one of nature's fools,' the marshal said with a grin, 'and I think that when Wes Brendel and some other fella came to take that wagon, you woke up from a drunken doze and recognized him. And he recognized you.'

The marshal stopped in mid-flight.

'Well, no,' he said softly. 'He'd have killed you there and then. He didn't even know you was on board, Fred, and when you got back to town, you tried pullin' a really fool trick.'

The old man's eyes narrowed.

'And what would that be, Marshal?' he asked cautiously.

'You went along to Wes – or his partner – and tried to get money. And that's why Wes paid you a visit. Who got hurt in your cabin, Fred? You or Wes?'

The old man's left hand instinctively went to the side of his left thigh. He stroked it gently.

'I was noddin' off when I heard him comin' in the door,' he muttered. 'It kinda scrapes on the ground a bit. It were dark but I could see him against the light from outside. He had a knife to finish me off quietly. I threw a whiskey jar and got him clean in the face. He went down on his knees so I grabbed my pants before he could get his wits together again. He made a lunge at me as I was leavin' the cabin and the knife caught me in the leg. Hurt real bad, it did. I belted him on the head with my Colt, but it fell out of my hand and I skedaddled before he could get to his feet again. I got away on my mule as fast as fast, but he couldn't follow me. He had no horse. I been here ever since.'

Luke glanced round the cabin. There was a cheap oil-lamp on a ledge and some food next to it. The blankets on the little cot were clean, and Fred was wearing a Colt .44 at his waist in what seemed to be a reasonably new belt.

'You appear to have picked up some money,' he said.

'Done a little work for local farmsteaders. Don't pay much but it lets me eat.'

'Who was the other fella with Wes?'

117

The old man shook his head vigorously.

'I didn't see him,' he said. 'He were just a blur in the darkness. But Wes drove the wagon and was real close. I coulda reached out and touched him.'

'Where's your mule and dog?'

'Round the back of this place, out of sight. I ain't headin' for town just yet, Marshal.'

'If I knew the name of Wes's partner,' the lawman said slowly, 'I could shove him in the jail-house and you'd be safe. But as long as he's free, you could get a bullet in the back just about any time. Who is he, Fred?'

'I don't know, and that's the truth, Marshal.' The man's voice had a note of desperation. 'If I did, I'd be happy to turn him in and go home again.'

'Fred, you got money from someone in town. Not off Wes. He wouldn't have the sort of cash that would buy what's round your waist and scattered round this cabin. You went to the boss man, and he paid up. And then he sent Wes to silence you. I want the name of that fella, because he's one dangerous man.'

Fred shook his head.

'I only saw Wes,' he insisted, 'and he gave me five dollars. The rest of it was in the wagon. I got me more than a hundred dollars, Marshal.'

The man's voice held a note of wonder at his own good fortune. He pulled a sheaf of bills from his pants pocket and showed it in a quivering hand to the surprised lawman.

'It was under the floor of the wagon,' he explained. 'I dropped one of the cases of liquor and it smashed a board. My foot went through it and I took a peek 'cos it seemed to have a hidin' place underneath. I could feel somethin' there, and pulled out this bundle of notes. I searched some more but there weren't nothin' else. This little bundle must have been left behind when they took the rest out, I figured. Well, it seemed to call for a drink, so I swallowed a few and then went off to sleep. Them fellas movin' the rig woke me up again, and it was then I recognized Wes Brendel. But that's why I can't go back to town, Marshal. Some fella is gonna claim I stole his money. And I've spent near half of it. Don't take me in, Marshal.'

'I ain't takin' you in, Fred,' Luke assured him, 'but I sure as hell need the name of the other fella with Wes. It'll be his money and I don't reckon to him claimin' it. Did you hear him speak? Or see his horse? Anythin' would help.'

The old man thought about it for a while. The assurance that he was not going to be taken back to town was making him more willing to co-operate.

'He were just a fella on a cow pony,' he said slowly. 'He did speak to Wes but it weren't nothin' distinct. Only thing I can tell you is that he didn't speak like Wes was his partner. More like a boss givin' orders. Know what I mean?'

'Yeah, I guess I do.'

119

Luke put his hand in his waistcoat pocket and pulled out five dollar coins.

'Give me one of the banknotes, Fred,' he said. 'They're a bit lighter to carry round than a heap of these.'

The old man handed one across and looked a bit suspiciously at the lawman. He was relieved when Luke got to his feet and indicated that he was leaving. He watched the marshal ride away before returning to his coffee to which he added a little whiskey just to improve the taste.

Huyton township was quiet for the next few days. With the saloon still closed and the recent funerals, there was a certain air of solemnity around. People glanced up at the beam above the grain-store as they passed. Some felt a slight guilt at the enthusiasm they had shown for the lynching of Cass Martin. The preacher found his church busier than usual, and took the opportunity to talk on the wages of sin in between choruses of the more popular hymns.

Luke Cassidy watched events quietly. An idea was gathering at the back of his mind and he was regretting the absence of a telegraph line between his office and Tombstone. There were things he needed to know, and so few people he could trust.

He went into the bank one morning when it was quiet. He had seen Dave Lundigan going down the street towards the mayor's store, and now approached the counter where an elderly teller

120

was writing in a large ledger. The scratching of his pen was loud and he looked up from his work with relief as the marshal placed a five-dollar bill on the counter.

'I got me a little law enforcement matter here,' the lawman said in a low, confidential voice. 'I'd like to have your experience on it, Amos.'

'If I can help, young Luke, be glad to do what I can.'

The man put the pen down with a certain thankfulness and adjusted the gold-rimmed glasses at the end of his beaky nose.

'Is this a real five-dollar bill?' the lawman asked.

The clerk gave him a calculating look and picked up the suspect article. He held it against the light, crumpled it a little between his fingers, and then took another note from a drawer to compare the two. He did everything with a slow, careful efficiency before finally making a pronouncement.

'It's a forgery, lad,' he said decisively. 'A good one, but as fake as a politician's promise. Where'd you get it?'

'Off a fella we suspect of passin' them in various towns,' Luke said vaguely. 'Have you seen any more around lately?'

The man shook his head.

'Nary a one,' he said, 'but if they're good 'uns like this and well-used, they could get circulated without too much trouble.'

'Thanks, Amos. This is strictly between you and

me. Law-enforcement business.'

The old man nodded as if glad to be part of the secret.

It was late afternoon when Mayor Kroner came out of the Harley House and crossed to his store. The more respectable members of the community were now using the hotel as a watering-hole while the saloon was closed. Drinks cost more and there was no gambling, but it was at least a meeting-place for the local businessmen and politicians.

Luke Cassidy watched him chat with Judge Mason before entering the building. He had sent Hal Levitt on another errand and was alone in the jailhouse. He picked up his hat and crossed the street to give the mayor some news that he felt he should have.

The town needed to be officially told that old Fred Brown was coming back to Huyton.

THIRTEEN

The old mule stood behind the rails of the corral and chewed away happily at the fodder in the trough. A mangy dog sat and scratched itself in the doorway of the cabin, while a thin wisp of smoke meandered up from the iron pipe at the side of the building.

Old Fred went in and out, doing odd jobs for the preacher, buying a few items of food in the main-street stores, and paying visits to the marshal's office.

Hal Levitt was installed there now, acting as a sort of unofficial deputy with the reluctant permission of the councilmen. He and Luke were sitting with coffee in front of them when Ma Harley arrived in a swirl of crisp petticoats. They rose to give her a chair and waited politely for her to state her business.

'I reckon as how it's about time I had that load of liquor sent over to my place,' she said without preamble. 'Business is mighty good at the moment, Marshal, and I may as well use that stuff just as my husband intended. Shame to leave it in storage while the saloon's closed. Perhaps old Fred will help tote it across the street for a dollar or two.'

Luke Cassidy stood by the stove, the coffee pot half-raised to pour her a cup of the steaming liquid.

'Now, that raises a problem, Ma,' he said slowly. 'You see, things have been happenin' around here that ain't explainable, and the mayor and the judge are mighty het up about it. Let's take that liquor now. It was used as a cover to bring some-thin' else into town. There's folks as think that whoever owns the liquor has some questions to answer.'

'Well, I know nothin' about any of that,' the woman said forcefully. 'My Bill simply bought it at auction and Wes Brendel did the hauling. If Wes was up to some other dirty work of his own, that ain't no business of mine. I just want that liquor delivered to the Harley House.'

'As I said, Ma,' the marshal went on as if she had not spoken, 'we have a real problem there. Bill Harley said he never bought no liquor. That's why he got hisself killed by Mosher. Then again, he never went to Tombstone hisself. It was Wes Brendel. The mayor has asked the judge to check the legal position in all this.'

'Banker Lundigan knows my Bill bought that liquor,' she snapped. 'They talked it over and that money-lending fella told you all about it.'

Luke nodded. 'That's a fact,' he said. 'Gave me it word for word, he did. But the judge wants an inquiry, so just let's leave it be for a few days, shall we?'

The woman stood up, looking angrily unde-cided for a moment. Then she stalked out of the office in a rustling of skirts that seemed to express her frustration.

'She sure as hell didn't like what you was sayin', Marshal.' Hal Levitt grinned.

'No, and there's a hell of a lot more she won't like in the near future.'

The moon had vanished behind dense cloud and the wind had dropped so that a total silence reigned over Huyton township. There was an occa-sional flap of wings as a bat flew low between the buildings to annoy the owls who were also on the hunt.

A shadowy figure moved quietly along a back lane and stopped as it neared the old cabin that Fred Brown occupied. The mule was silent and the old dog slept heavily after a meal that had been dosed with laudanum by the same visitor as had paid it an earlier call. The figure moved towards the door of the cabin and listened.

The place was in darkness and the iron pipe of the stove was cool to the touch. The shadowy figure lifted the door carefully on its leather hinges and moved it just a few inches. A vague form could be seen on the narrow cot, hunched against the wall. As the watcher's eyes grew accustomed to the darkness of the place, he could see the whiskey jug at the side of the cot and a shotgun lying near it.

He opened the door a little more until he could slip through and move quietly across the earthen floor. There was a small axe in his hand now and he struck savagely at the figure in the cot. The blows rained down in quick succession until the assailant suddenly realized that something was wrong.

He pulled back the bedclothes and grabbed the figure that should now be pouring blood from a shattered skull. All he had in front of him was a straw-filled dummy with a pumpkin head.

He let out an audible curse, dropped the axe and fled from the scene, running down the back lane and scattering foraging rats in his path.

Luke Cassidy was in the little cabin with old Fred at his side. Hal Levitt stood in the doorway, and the three of them surveyed the straw dummy and the axe that lay on the floor. Fred Brown looked shattered.

'That could have been you, old-timer,' Luke said quietly. 'This fella ain't playin' games. Do you understand that now?'

The old man nodded dumbly.

'Will my dog be all right?' he asked.

'The horse-doctor reckons as how he was fed meat with laudanum in it. He'll survive. Which is more than you would have done. Now, ain't it about time you told me who the fella was with the wagon that night?'

'I don't know nothing, Marshal,' the old man said stubbornly.

'Look, Fred,' the lawman explained patiently, 'you saw both fellas with that wagon, and when you got back to town, you tried to get money out of the boss-man. He paid up, but then he sent Wes to kill you. You ain't safe while he's still around, and he ain't never goin' to give you any more money. You're the only one who knows who he is, and he don't aim you should go talkin' to the law.'

'You got me into this mess,' Fred snapped angrily. 'Threatenin' to put a poor old fella into jail for the sake of a few forged five dollar bills. I didn't know they was forged. How could I? I wanna leave town, Marshal. I'm scared.'

'Then let me grab the fella behind all this. I already think I know who it is, but the judge needs someone to identify him and tie him in with that wagon. Come on, Fred, there's a reward involved, and I reckon as how you'd never be short of food and drink for the rest of your life.'

It was the thought of drink rather than food that turned the tables. Fred told them who the man was.

*

It was close to noon and the bank was quite busy when Luke Cassidy and Mayor Kroner put in an appearance. People stared at them, as if the very fact that they were together made it some sort of official visit.

Old Amos looked up from his work, and when his customer departed, he came across to the end of the counter to speak to the two men.

'Is Mr Lundigan in his office?' the mayor asked.

'No, he's had to go to a meetin' in Tombstone,' the chief clerk told him. 'Left early this mornin' in his rig and won't be back for two or three days. Left me the keys, he did.'

'Seems a bit sudden,' the First Citizen said. 'He never mentioned it to me.'

The old man smiled sadly. 'Mr Lundigan near forgot it, Mayor,' he explained. 'Came round to my house first thing this mornin' in a fine old fret, he did. Told me that he'd misread the date on the letter and that the meetin' was real important. Never did see him so almighty flustered.'

'I can imagine,' Luke said drily. 'Have you checked your money supply, Amos?'

The chief clerk blinked so hard that his glasses fell off and dangled from their cord.

'Why should I be doin' that?' he asked in bewilderment.

'Well, when bank presidents leave town in a hurry, they often take all the ready cash with them. It's an old custom.'

The man stared at Luke for a moment and then

128

seemed to think it a good joke.

'Oh, we ain't got that sort of trouble, Marshal,' he laughed. 'All our money checks against the books. I keep proper control over things like that.'

'Glad to hear it.'

The lawman looked around the bank. There were only two customers at the counter now and he pulled the chief clerk aside.

'Let's go into the office,' he suggested quietly.

The man nodded and led the way unresistingly to the small room with its large green safe and imposing rolltop desk.

'You think something's gone wrong, young fella,' the old man said as he pulled open the door of the safe, 'but I check the money every morning, automatic-like. Been doin' it for so many years, I'd know instantly if there was somethin' fishy. Mr Lundigan ain't no thief, lad. He's as honest as the day is long.'

Marshal Cassidy stood in front of the safe and looked at the bundles of paper money. He picked up a wad of five-dollar bills and handed it to the chief clerk.

'Are they genuine?' he asked.

The man took the bills and stared at them for a moment. He was almost on the verge of saying that he had no doubts in the matter, but noticed the expressions on the faces of his two companions.

He took them over to the window and started perusing and feeling the notes carefully. He held some of them up to the light and Luke noticed that his liver-spotted hand was beginning to tremble.

'They're all forgeries,' he said at last.

FOURTEEN

The mayor hammered on the door of the smartly painted house on the outskirts of Huyton township. There were neat windows, curtained with yellow lace, a small garden with gravelled path, and a large cat sitting on the step.

Mrs Lundigan came at once to open it and hastily admitted her visitors. She seemed anxious to usher them into the house before the neighbours saw that she was getting what looked like an official visit from the law.

The room into which the marshal and the mayor were shown was as smart as the outside of the building. A large Turkey carpet covered the floor, an Eli Wood clock ticked away on the wall, and a large Chicago-built organ occupied one corner. The place smelled of lavender and the curtains were drawn back to admit as much light as possible.

Mrs Lundigan was a small woman, stout and plainly dressed. She looked as if she had been crying and the hand that waved the men to the neatly tapestried chairs was trembling slightly.

'I know why you're here,' she said in a taut voice, 'but he's long gone and taken it all with him.'

The mayor spoke before Luke Cassidy could say anything.

'Just tell us all about it, Maggie,' he urged. 'We got real trouble on our hands here.'

She sat down opposite them and twisted the edge of the apron in her hands.

'I know what it's all about,' she admitted. 'Dave has been acting bad this last year or so. It happened after he made a trip to Tombstone for a bank meeting. December it was, and when he came back home, he was like he'd won first prize out of the cracker barrel. He wouldn't tell me much, but he was certain sure that we'd be rich one day and leaving small towns behind us. I figured as how he was talking promotion at first; then things started happening.'

She stopped and looked aimlessly around the room. Her eyes were brimming over as she came back to the subject.

'I eventually found out what he was doing,' she went on. 'He'd met some fella again in Tombstone whom he'd known years back. This fella was a forger and made himself rich during the war. He sold the forged money to banking men like Dave, who would then feed it bit by bit through the system. They were good forgeries and he'd never been caught. Dave started doing the same thing here. He bought the notes at a discount and swapped them a few at a time through the bank. He swore it was easier than shooting fish in a barrel.'

She sniffed and searched in her pocket for a handkerchief.

'Wes Brendel made the trips to Tombstone to pick up the dud notes and pay for them. Dave didn't trust him, but he was the only person in town he could use. Then something went wrong.'

She paused again and Luke butted in to try and assert his authority.

'The Tombstone lawmen started askin' questions,' he suggested.

'Yes.' She nodded.

'I been checkin' with Marshal Earp,' Luke went on, 'and he tells me that the federal folks are gettin' real worried about this forgin' business. He's huntin' out every likely fella in his area who might be involved in forgery. So they had to move everythin' out of town. Right?'

She nodded again. 'Yes, that's it. Dave got a message that this fella needed help to move his paper, the metal plates, and a lot of new money out of town as soon as possible. Dave agreed to help him and sent Wes to Tombstone to do the job.'

'What about the printin' press?' asked Mayor Kroner.

'That was well hidden, and the man was a storekeeper in Tombstone and highly respected. The marshal there was more suspicious of the local printers and newspaper offices. While he wasted time checking on them, the forging fella decided to move things out of town before it was his turn to be visited by the law.'

'And the load of liquor?' Luke asked.

'Dave read in the Tombstone papers that a hotel had failed and was putting its stuff up for auction. He hired a wagon off Chris Beatty and sent Wes into Tombstone to bid for the stuff. But you know Wes.'

The two men nodded. They knew Wes.

'And what trick did he play?' the marshal enquired.

'Dave gave him a bank-draft made out in the name of Bill Harley. That was in case anything went wrong. Wes got the liquor, moved it on to the wagon, and then should have quietly picked up the other stuff from the forger, hidden it in the secret compartment, and come quietly back here. But he had to be the smart one.'

She shook her head angrily and Luke Cassidy began to doubt her innocence in what had happened.

'The tarnation fool was driving the rig down behind this gun-store, and he decided to do a little business on the side. He broke in, loaded up the guns, and headed out of town. Dave had arranged to meet him near Taranga Rocks, and by the time the wagon got there, the horse was near-dead with the weight he had to haul. Dave was real furious and told him to dump the guns in the cactus and stick to what they'd arranged. Then they drove to Dead Man's Canyon, turned the horse loose, and unloaded the money and plates. They left the liquor until the next day so that it could be brought into town all innocent-like. But that preacher fella took a short cut.'

Luke nodded as he considered her story.

'And the mayor here spoiled things by insistin' I go out and bring the wagon into town?' he mused.

She managed a slight smile.

'Dave couldn't risk that,' she said. 'He and Wes rode out hell for leather. They didn't care about the liquor but they couldn't have anybody looking too close at the rig. Not with that hiding-place under the boards.'

'And I reckon that Dave must have had quite a scare when old Fred turned up at the back door tryin' to screw some money out of him,' Luke said quietly.

The woman shook her head sadly.

'That's where it all went wrong,' she admitted. 'Dave gave him a few dollars, and the old man would have been quite happy with an occasional hand-out. But he was a drunk, and drunks talk.'

'So your husband sent Wes to kill him?' the mayor asked.

'Yes.' Her voice was very low and she no longer looked the two men in the eyes.

'Tell us the rest, Ma,' the mayor prompted eagerly.

'Well, Fred got away and Dave was real worried

that he might go to the marshal. He decided that the wagon would have to be destroyed. So he told Wes to hire it from Phil Breen. Then Wes drove it out of town, met Dave, and they poured lamp-oil over it and set it alight. And Dave killed Wes.'

'Why?' the mayor asked.

She shrugged. 'He said it was because Wes demanded more money, but I reckon it was just to make sure he didn't talk.'

'Sounds about right,' Luke said drily, 'and when I brought old Fred into town, I reckon your husband musta got real worried.'

'He did. He wasn't sure what Fred would do. Whether he'd be content with more money, or whether he'd talk to the law. So he slipped out early this morning with a hunk of meat and some of my laudanum mixture. I'm not habitual with it, you understand; just take it to get a good night's sleep now and then. Then he came back, waited another hour or so, and went off again. I didn't know what he was aiming to do.'

She did not sound very convincing and the two men waited silently for the rest of the story.

'He was in a real state when he returned. Scared white he was, and started hitching the surrey like the devil was on his tail. He told me what had happened. Fred was not at the cabin and there was a straw dummy there. He reckoned that he'd walked into a trap and he lit out of here faster than a scalded cat.'

She seemed to cheer up at the scene she

conjured and even managed a nervous little titter.

'But he cleared us out,' she went on. 'The no-good son of Satan took every cent in the house. I'm flat broke, Marshal. Left with nothing after twenty or more years of slaving for him.'

Luke and the mayor glanced at each other but there was no sympathy in their eyes.

'You got this place,' Mayor Kroner said unkindly, 'and there's his ridin'-horse out in the corral. And you got young Eddie. Now, that's a fine lad there, Maggie, even if he is trainin' to be a lawyer.'

'He's gone too,' she snapped, realizing that no sympathy was coming her way.

'You mean that he took off with his father?' the mayor asked in wonderment.

'No, he's a good lad, as you said. He took after Dave with a gun.'

Eddie Lundigan was a slight young man, barely eighteen and dressed like the lawyer he aimed to be. His horse was a light-footed roan gelding that bore his weight easily as he moved across the sparse grass towards the west. He would have been handsome had it not been for the large beaked nose that dominated his thin face. He looked immature under the dark hat and with the black stock that stood out against a neatly laundered white shirt.

There was a gun at his waist and a belt full of .44 cartridges. The Colt was an early model, fired many times as he had practised since buying it from Drugget's store without telling his father. He was a good shot, used to the kick of the weapon as he drew fast the way his heroes did in the stories to be found in the dime library.

He felt betrayed. His father was running off: a wanted man, a criminal who had deserted his wife and son. He had disgraced the family name and left young Eddie to live down the scandal that must follow. The young man did not know the whole story, but his father was a killer, had robbed the bank, and gone off with every cent they had in the house.

Eddie wanted revenge. He was going to stand up to trouble for the first time in his life and prove himself to the community. If he got back the bank's cash, he would be a hero. His future in the law business would be assured, and maybe he could be mayor of Huyton township one day. Dave Lundigan had always looked upon his son as a pantywaist, and he was going to be proved wrong.

Eddie knew the trail to follow. His father would be headed for the old Gardner spread, some fifty miles west of Huyton. His widowed sister lived there with three sons and several cowpokes. Dave Lundigan would be out of Marshal Cassidy's territory and well surrounded by friendly guns. Eddie meant to stop him reaching the safety of his sister's home.

He sweated under the sun and with the unaccustomed exercise as he licked his lips to take away the crust of red dust that gathered there. He began to come to his senses as he rode. The mind of a cold and calculating lawyer began to take over from the first wild thoughts that had sent him on his errand. There were questions to be faced.

Would his father tamely surrender when faced with a gun? Would there be a shoot-out? And trickiest of all, who would win? His pace almost slowed as he thought about that last one. His father might be a money-lender encased in an office all day, but he was no stranger to firearms and always carried a Derringer. He also kept a .44 Smith & Wesson at the bank. As deadly a weapon as the Colt that Eddie carried at his hip.

And then another question came to his fevered mind. Could he shoot his father if it came to the point? He tried to brush away the thought and dug his spurs into the startled horse to move it faster across the uneven trail.

Dave Lundigan had taken the surrey and loaded all his clothes and other personal items aboard it. He was travelling slowly, scared of breaking the wheel-spokes if he went too fast. He was sweating as much as his son was, but it was fear that was making him perspire so much. It was no longer a matter of prison for passing dud money. It was a morning date with the hangman, if he was lucky enough not to be lynched like the bounty hunter.

His sister and her sons would keep him safe. If strangers came on to their range, he would get enough warning to flee across the border. As the miles passed, he began to cheer up a little. His fool of a wife and pantywaist son had already been forgotten, and he almost began to look forward to a life without them. The engraved plates he carried were worth a great deal of money. He had nearly all the bank's cash, his own savings, and a pile of counterfeit notes that could be passed in small quantities for years to come. He also had his wife's jewellery. He had been lavish with presents to her in their younger days, and now his kindness was paying off.

His mood lightened as he steered the rig carefully along a gully. He slowed down a little. Nobody would be pursuing him, and it was good to smell the air and feel the slight breeze that came off the distant hills. He would rest soon near a shallow stream that would supply him with water for strong coffee. He started to hum one of his favourite tunes as he drove. It did not strike him as ironic that it was a hymn.

The rig emerged from the gully and climbed up to the higher ground which would lead to a long, sloping plain of yellowish grass and tall cacti. He sighed contentedly as he glanced to the rear to get his bearings from the sun.

There was a dark cloud on the horizon. It was a mass of red dust that sprayed across the ground and heralded the approach of a horseman. Dave Lundigan cursed and looked around desperately for somewhere to hide himself and the surrey. The ground was too open and he decided to make a run for it.

He shouted to the horse, cracked the reins across its back, and the rig speeded up, creating its own cloud of dust which could be seen for several miles.

The surrey lumbered over the ground, bouncing on thick bushes, its wheels grinding against gravel and rocks as it lurched dangerously. One of his carpetbags bounced off and had to be left on the ground. He hoped that it only contained clothes, but there was not time to find out. He had to outdistance the horseman.

And then it happened. One of the wheels hit a larger piece of rock and the rig bounced a couple of feet off the ground. He heard the wooden spokes shatter and saw the iron rim shoot off to rest among a clump of mesquite. The surrey fell over on its side, the hub digging into the earth and acting as a brake. Dave Lundigan pulled on the reins. He knew that there was nothing that could be done now. He was on foot.

The horse came thankfully to a halt as the driver jumped off the rig and unholstered the large Smith & Wesson pistol. He checked the load and waited in sweaty defiance for the rider to appear.

There was not long to wait. It was the roan gelding that he recognized first. Dave Lundigan breathed a sigh of relief. It was only that young milksop of a lad, riding the range dressed like a hair-splitting lawyer. He put the gun away and stood by his horse, his hand resting on its flank to steady it after the long drive and the presence of another animal.

'Well, lad, and have you come to join your dear old pa on his new adventures?' he asked cheerfully as Eddie reined in.

'I've come for Ma's jewellery,' the young man answered firmly as he dismounted. 'And all the money you stole. I aim to have it, Pa, so let's not waste time being polite.'

Dave Lundigan found it difficult to repress a smile.

'Well, there's a brave lad I raised,' he mocked. 'Let me tell you something, young fella. You and your ma can fend for yourselves from now on. I've fed and clothed you both, gave you everything you could wish for, but now I got problems. So, you're out of my life. I suggest you just turn your horse around and go safe home. You wouldn't want me to spank you now, would you?'

Eddie flushed angrily and his hand went to the gun at his waist. His father was taken by surprise. That was something he had never expected. He dived for his own weapon as he dodged for safety along the flank of his horse.

Eddie's shot took the animal in the side of the head and it reared in terror before falling over on its side. The surrey was dragged with it as the animal kicked amid a tangle of harness.

Dave Lundigan fired back at his son but the rearing of the horse upset his aim and the shot went wide. Both men recocked their pistols and fired again. They were only a few feet apart and it had to be a duel to the death.

FIFTEEN

Mrs Lundigan had told the marshal where her husband would be heading. She had no more loyalty towards him and was worried about her son. Luke Cassidy rode at a steady pace towards the ranch that was legally beyond his range and where he would be alone against a mass of fire-power.

He had left Hal Levitt as his deputy and travelled lightly, with a small bag of food and a couple of water-skins. His only real hope of catching Dave Lundigan lay in the fact that the man was older than he was, was hampered by driving a surrey, and might meet up with his own son.

Luke could not be sure what would happen then. He found it hard to imagine the vapid young man using a gun, but he had no doubt that the banker would not hesitate to kill anybody who tried to take away his wealth and lead him to a gallows.

Dave Lundigan had several hours' start and Luke tried to make up for it by moving his horse at a steady pace. He needed to make as much distance as possible before dusk, and must then hope that the sky would be clear for the moon to guide him during the night. He knew that it was no use looking for a trail. The wind blew all traces from the gritty earth, and all he could rely on was the well-worn route across the range that meandered from watering-hole to watering-hole in the general direction of the ranch he was heading for.

It was late-afternoon when he came upon a lone horse. It was a roan gelding, saddled and bridled. It was away to his right, grazing peacefully off a clump of tall grass. He approached carefully and the animal looked up in curiosity as he neared it. Its reins were hanging loose and touching the ground. He hoped that it had the instincts of a cow pony and would regard itself as being tethered in that position. He hesitated to approach and decided to dismount and let his own animal do the work for him.

He got down from the saddle, gave his horse a gentle tap on the rump and let it wander over to the clump of grass and the company of another creature more to its liking than a human being.

The two animals nuzzled each other and then concentrated on eating. Luke was able to join them and collect the reins of both without any trouble. He knew who the horse belonged to. He had seen Eddie Lundigan riding it many times, and now its rider was missing.

He remounted, took the other animal in tow, and continued the journey. He was more hopeful now. Something had happened and whatever it was, Dave Lundigan must have been delayed for a time. He scanned the horizon in vain for any clouds of dust and pressed on through a small gully and out on to higher ground with a wide sweep of grassland ahead of him.

And then he spotted the surrey, the dead horse, and the man who lay against a clump of bushes with his hand resting on a pistol. It was Dave Lundigan.

Luke Cassidy halted the horses and unholstered his shotgun. He was going to play for safety. He looked for Eddie and eventually saw a pair of feet sticking out from behind the overturned surrey. Eddie Lundigan was dead.

'You don't need a gun, Marshal!' The banker's voice was loud in the emptiness of the vast range. 'I'm not shooting anybody else today.'

He almost laughed as he said it, throwing the large pistol from him and spreading out his blood-stained hands in a gesture of submission. Luke Cassidy could see why they were bloodstained.

Dave Lundigan had received a bullet just above the waistline and the blood was oozing through his shirt and down his dark pants.

The lawman reholstered the shotgun and got down from his mount. He tethered the two animals to a bush and approached the wounded man a little warily.

'You hurt bad, Mr Lundigan?' he asked.

'Bad enough to die, lad,' the man said cheerfully, 'and funnily enough, I don't seem to mind somehow. I've lain here for two hours now, not feeling anything much, but sorta dozing now and then. Being content. It's a strange thing, Marshal, but the money doesn't mean anything any more. And coming from a man who's spent all his life with money, that's one hell of a confession.'

He pointed a slightly trembling hand towards the surrey.

'You'll find the plates and the counterfeit notes in that black leather bag,' he said. 'All the real cash money is in my pockets. And my wife's jewellery. I guess everything I did was a waste of time. You knew it was me, didn't you?'

Luke glanced round as if looking for inspiration in the desolate wilderness.

'I certainly can't get you to a doctor,' he murmured, 'and you can't ride a horse in that condition. There ain't a lot we can do.'

The man nodded. 'I know that,' he muttered. 'It was all a waste. I didn't start out meaning to kill folk, but when you're in deep, there ain't a lot of choice. Old Fred was a danger, and Wes Brendel demanded more money at every turn of the card.'

'And your son?'

Dave Lundigan sighed.

'I have to hand it to the lad. I never thought he had it in him. I didn't expect him to have the guts to draw on me. And I'm rather proud of him in a way. Will you do me just one favour, Marshal?'

'What is it?'

'Just stay with me to the end. I don't think I'll delay you too long, but I'd rather not be alone.'

Dave Lundigan lasted another two hours and the sun had set by the time he closed his eyes peacefully as if sleeping. Luke Cassidy bedded down for the night, made himself a meal, and slept surprisingly well until daylight struck him in the eyes and he woke to another hot and dry day.

There was nothing he could do with the bodies except leave them to the elements. He found the plates, all the money, real and forged, and also a stack of paper for making new notes. He collected the guns, everything else of value, and loaded it all across the spare horse in the various carpetbags.

He was an hour's ride from a small creek and stopped there to get more water. Then it was simply a matter of making his way at a steady pace to Huyton township.

SIXTEEN

The town was in festive mood when Luke Cassidy returned with the bank's money. He was the hero of the hour and nobody was very much concerned that Dave Lundigan and his son were dead. After all, one had been a money-lender and the other threatened to become a lawyer.

The saloon was due to open again. Mosher's son had arrived with his family to settle in and keep the place flourishing as in the past. If Ma Harley's nose was put out of joint by the news, she still managed to switch on an inviting smile as she welcomed the more respectable drinkers to the refinement of her hotel.

The marshal was there as the guest of the mayor and the rest of the town personalities. Since the festivities were being held in a hotel, their wives were also being entertained, and Ella sat demurely next to the judge's wife while her husband was fêted for what he had achieved. Nobody mentioned a reward but they all knew that their marshal was going to be on the receiving end of quite a sum of money.

Old Fred was also there. He was not classified as one of the respectable members of the community, but Ma Harley had made an exception in view of the risk he had taken to lure Dave Lundigan into an attempted murder.

'What interests me,' the mayor said as they sat around an elegant mahogany table, 'is why you suspected Dave. I'd have put him down as one real solid citizen.'

The judge nodded agreement. Nodding was about all he could manage after what he had drunk.

'I suppose it was because I believed Bill Harley,' Luke said. 'He swore that he never bought that liquor, and when Dave Lundigan told me that Bill Harley had arranged the deal through him, then one of them had to be a liar. And I picked Dave Lundigan.'

The mayor nodded. 'And that's why you told us that old Fred was comin' back to town?' he asked.

'Yes. Fred knew too much and was a drunk. I reckoned as how he'd have to be killed. So I paraded the old fella all around town, sent him out to his cabin to make up the straw dummy, and then just waited to see if Dave Lundigan took the bait. He sure as hell did.'

'And where did old Fred really spend the night?' the mayor asked.

'In the jailhouse. Safest place in town.' The lawman grinned.

150

They all laughed and the noise attracted Ma Harley who came across with another bottle of whiskey.

'Well, Marshal,' she said with a certain authority, 'now that all the fuss is over, I reckon I'll be takin' my liquor out of storage in the next day or so. Old Fred can shift it when he sobers up.'

The mayor winked at Luke and gave the dozing judge a nudge.

'I don't see as how that's possible, Ma,' he said in his official mayoral voice.

'And why not? My Bill bought it fair and square. I got me a copy of the receipt.'

'That's true, but it was Dave Lundigan who bought the liquor and used Bill's name. And it was Wes Brendel who helped him. Your husband was tellin' the truth when he denied havin' bought that load of drinks. So the liquor is now the property of the town of Huyton to be auctioned off to aid public funds.'

'Public funds, my Aunt Martha!' the genteel hotel owner screeched. 'I own that liquor fair and square.'

'To own that liquor, ma'am, you'd have to be the accomplice to passin' stolen bills, one killing, and one attempted killing. Ain't I right, Marshal?'

'I reckon so,' Luke Cassidy said, trying to keep a straight face. 'Of course, the judge will have the last say.'

They all looked at the representative of the judiciary as he straightened up, placed his glasses on the end of his nose, and nodded with amiable acknowledgement.

Ma Harley turned on her heel and stormed away to tell her daughters not to serve any more free drinks at that table.

Friday was an overcast day with a threat of seasonal rain. The Golden Chance was again open for business and old Fred was employed in the job of bringing the load of liquor out of the jailhouse and piling it case by case, jar by jar at the side of a small wheeled rostrum that had been brought out for the auctioneer.

Fred was happy in his work, even after having to surrender the last of the five-dollar bills that Dave Lundigan had overlooked in the wagon.

The auctioneer usually dealt in cattle, and the rostrum had been wheeled from the stockyards at the far end of town. It brought something of its aroma with it, but the man who would mount the creaking wooden timbers was an image of elegance.

Sam Basset was a dandy. A fat dandy, it's true, but a man whose bright waistcoat, well-cut suits, and grey silk stocks earned him glances from middle-aged ladies. He wore a stovepipe hat that was tilted airily on the back of his head to display as much as possible of the wavy grey hair. His red face was perpetually smiling and the cigar that adorned his full mouth emitted a cloud of Cuban delight.

The liquor had been divided up into small lots, each one labelled and the whole drawn up in a catalogue. Sam had advised his fellow councilmen that, sold as smaller portions, the liquor was likely to bring in more money. None of them was going to argue about that point. The council would be controlling the money, and more than one member was already thinking about a bit of new furniture or some items of clothing from his share.

Luke Cassidy was trying to supervise old Fred. He knew that several jars of the cheaper whiskey had already gone astray, and with each journey to and from the jailhouse, the old drunk's walk seemed more erratic. Fred was doing a pretty good job under the circumstances, but some of the brandy was valuable and Luke eyed the proceedings with distinct unease. Hal Levitt was lending a hand. He had been confirmed as a deputy and was eager to show some public spirit.

The main street was crowded as the time neared for the auction. The preacher stayed away as a mark of his disfavour, or possibly because nobody had suggested that he be given a share of the profits. Except for that, the turnout was large. Almost as large as could normally be expected for a hanging. Mayor Kroner looked on happily, hoping that some of the women would persuade their husbands to buy some foreign spirits that would show their social superiority.

The auctioneer came out of the jailhouse at two o'clock precisely. He was like an actor taking the stage, with a radiant smile and a cigar clasped between his full lips. His clerk followed with a bundle of papers while the crowd raised applause as for the opening of a show. Sam Basset held up an elegant, beringed hand for silence as he read out the rules of the auction. He used the same routine as when he sold cattle, but nobody seemed to notice. He picked up the catalogue, glanced round his appreciative audience, and made his decisive announcement.

'The auction will now begin!'

A ragged cheer went up and some cowpoke at the back of the crowd let out a yodelling shriek and fired his pistol in the air. Old Fred also drew his gun, waved it uncertainly about his head, and then fired his own salute.

The fact that he fell over while he was doing it and actually shot an expensive bottle of brandy which was in a crate with eleven others, only produced uproarious applause from the crowd. Luke stopped laughing long enough to guide the old man away to the wooden stoop so that he could sit against the hitching rail without falling down again.

Even the auctioneer managed a smile and then held up his hand for silence once again. He took out his cigar to address the audience.

'Now, folks,' he shouted in his resonant voice, 'let us get down to the business of sellin' this magnificent collection of fine spirits to those folk who appreciate a real good drop of liquor. We will start with lot number one. A case of genuine Scotch whisky that is being pointed out by my assistant here.'

Sam Basset waved his hand in the direction of his helper, and as the man touched the wooden case of liquor, the auctioneer shoved the cigar back in his mouth, exuded a plume of fragrant smoke, then placed it on the edge of the desk while he gathered in the bids. They came at a brisk rate and his hand darted from face to face as he took in each offer. Then, with gavel wavering, he drew out one final bid and brought down the small mallet with a crash on the desk top.

What happened next was to be the talk of Huyton township for many years to come. The vibration made the cigar jump in the air and tumble off the rostrum. It rolled across the ground and lay amid a pool of liquid before bursting into flames. It had landed in the spilt brandy and the flames shot up the sides of the wooden case.

Luke Cassidy leapt forward but was impeded by more sensible people who were leaping backwards. Bottles began to burst with the heat, showering glass and brandy around the pile of crates and jars. The auctioneer fled from the rostrum while his assistant was busy trying to rescue what he could.

Fred wanted to save a few items as well, but fell down before he could reach the liquor. Viewed from a safe distance, the townsfolk were now happily watching a scene that, for a few old people, was to be compared with the burning of Atlanta.

The mayor looked on in despair as the flames mounted and the contents of the whiskey wagon vanished as swiftly as they had appeared.